"Dammit, Woman,"

Adam erupted, "we have no past. I have never met you, don't know you, and you sure as hell can't know me."

"Oh, but I do," Sunny persisted, meeting his narrow-eyed glare with fearless composure. "I would know you anywhere."

"How do you know me?" he insisted. "How, when we have never met, never seen each other?"

"Not in this lifetime, no," she agreed.

Oh, hell, Adam thought savagely, seeing his hopes for a mutually satisfying holiday dalliance growing dimmer with each statement she made. He, Adam Grainger, so selective about his female companions, was attracted—strongly attracted—to a cuckoo bird!

Dear Reader,

A book from Joan Hohl is always a delight, so I'm thrilled that this month we have her latest MAN OF THE MONTH, *A Memorable Man*. Naturally, this story is chock-full of Joan's trademark sensuality *and* it's got some wonderful plot twists that are sure to please you!

Also this month, Cindy Gerard's latest in her NORTHERN LIGHTS BRIDES series, *A Bride for Crimson Falls*, and Beverly Barton's "Southern sizzle" is highlighted in *A Child of Her Own*. Anne Eames has the wonderful ability to combine sensuality and humor, and *A Marriage Made in Joeville* features this talent.

The Baby Blizzard by Caroline Cross is sure to melt your heart this month—it's an extraordinary love story with a hero and heroine you'll never forget! And the month is completed with a sexy romp by Diana Mars, *Matchmaking Mona*.

In months to come, look for spectacular Silhouette Desire books by Diana Palmer, Jennifer Greene, Lass Small and many other fantastic Desire stars! And I'm always here to listen to your thoughts and opinions about the books. You can write to me at the address below.

Enjoy! I wish you hours of happy reading!

Lucia Macro

Lucia Macro
Senior Editor

Please address questions and book requests to:
Silhouette Reader Service
U.S.: 3010 Walden Ave., P.O. Box 1325, Buffalo, NY 14269
Canadian: P.O. Box 609, Fort Erie, Ont. L2A 5X3

JOAN HOHL
A MEMORABLE MAN

SILHOUETTE *Desire*®
Published by Silhouette Books
America's Publisher of Contemporary Romance

SILHOUETTE BOOKS

ISBN 0-373-76075-2

A MEMORABLE MAN

Copyright © 1997 by Joan Hohl

Printed in U.S.A.

Books by Joan Hohl

JOAN HOHL

is the bestselling author of almost three dozen books. She has received numerous awards for her work, including the Romance Writers of America Golden Medallion Award. In addition to contemporary romance, this prolific author also writes historical and time-travel romances. Joan lives in eastern Pennsylvania with her husband and family.

To my editor, Melissa Senate,
for being such a nice bully

One

It was fascinating, like stepping back over two hundred years in time.

Bemused by the novelty of the experience, Adam Grainger came to an abrupt halt behind the two elderly ladies blocking his passage to Duke of Gloucester Street. In no particular hurry, instead of circling around them, he waited patiently for them to finish their conversation and then either cross the street or part company.

It had been snowing when Adam flew out of Wyoming that morning, snowing and windy and bitterly cold. Rather normal weather for mid-December. At the time, since he was flying toward the eastern seaboard, he had presumed it would be cold in Virginia, as well.

But it wasn't cold; in fact with the temperature hovering around 62°, the air felt balmy against his face.

While waiting, basking in the gentle sunshine, Adam slowly took in his surroundings, the sights and sounds of the restored capital city of Colonial Williamsburg, Virginia.

Lowering his gaze to his hands, he studied the well-marked map, which delineated every street and restored building in the area. His bearings set, he raised his eyes. Directly opposite, across the cobbled street, stood the Bruton Parish Church, and beyond the church, the Governor's Palace rose majestically at the end of the two-block-long Palace Green.

But it wasn't the lovely old church or even the more imposing palace in the background that caught Adam's attention and fancy, riveting his gaze.

A young woman was approaching the street from the green. Although attired in the period costume of a reenactor, she strode forth with the free and easy long-legged gait of the modern woman, a long dark red cape swirling around her ankles, a mobcap swinging by its strings from her fingers. Sunlight glimmered in loosened strands of gold streaking her brown hair, which was gathered into a carelessly fashioned topknot.

An odd sensation of familiarity flared to life inside Adam. Startled by the feeling, he stood staring, arrested by the very sight of her beautiful composed face.

"A pity, really, she's such a lovely girl."

Adam couldn't help but overhear the remark made by one of the ladies standing less than a foot in front of him. A movement of the lady's head indicated the remark had obviously been intended to apply to the young woman coming to a halt at the opposite curb.

A pity? he thought, frowning. What could there be to feel pity for such an enchanting creature? The thought had no sooner struck him than the answer was forthcoming.

"A bit odd, you know," the lady murmured in a sympathetic tone, shaking her head.

"So I've heard," the other lady replied, heaving a sigh. "Although she seems fine most of the time, I understand she is subject to moments of delusions or some such."

The first lady nodded in agreement. "Not only that," she informed sadly. "But I've been told she goes off on rather wild and strange flights of fancy."

Delusions? Wild and strange flights of fancy? Containing an urge to laugh aloud, Adam shot a glance at the woman under discussion. Although the woman hesitated near the curb, her expression of growing consternation seemed merely to indicate mild indecisiveness. She certainly didn't ap-

pear to Adam as either odd or given to sudden wild
and strange flights of fancy.

At that instant, just as Adam heard the two ladies say their goodbyes and separate, the woman
stepped off the curb and into the street. Adam did
likewise, strolling toward her as she strode toward
him. As they drew alongside one another he felt
another decidedly strange jolt, at the same time
noting the sudden widening of her eyes.

What the hell?

Even as the thought flashed through his mind,
Adam was brought up short by the sound of her
voice.

"Andrew?"

A case of mistaken identity. Surprised by the
sharp sense of disappointment he felt, Adam
turned to offer her a small smile and a reluctant
disclaimer.

"Sorry, but no, I am—"

"No, of course not." She smiled, raised her
eyes, and sighed, as if impatient with herself.
"You wouldn't be Andrew. Not again."

Huh? Clueless, Adam stood there, right in the
middle of Duke of Gloucester Street, not only
speechless but dumbfounded to the point of being
oblivious to the horse-drawn wagon lumbering toward them.

"Oh, dear, after all this time, you still don't
know, do you?" She sighed again, then, before he
could think of a reply or even so much as how to

reply, she glanced beyond him and grasped his arm. "Come along," she urged, leading him back the way he had come from the other side of the street. "We're in danger of being run down here."

Run down? Adam frowned, but nevertheless moved at her bidding. Surely the woman knew better than most that vehicular traffic wasn't allowed within the restored area? His silent query was answered the next moment, when the tourist-laden wagon rumbled by, missing them by a mere foot or so.

Well, damn, he reflected, staring in bemusement at the horses and rough-hewn conveyance. He couldn't recall seeing anything about the availability of wagon rides in the packet he'd been given at the visitors' center. Of course, at the time, wanting to experience the place for himself, rather than read about it, he had given the information little more than a casual perusal.

"It's a wagon," he said, unnecessarily, and more to himself than to the woman standing beside him...now well out of harm's way. "A horse-drawn wagon."

"I know."

The thread of amused understanding woven through her voice snagged Adam's attention. Forgetting the wagon, he turned to level a probing look at her. "What did you mean earlier, when you said I wouldn't be Andrew again?"

"Well, you wouldn't, would you?" she replied, her smile enigmatic and knowing.

Knowing what? Adam wondered, frowning. She was a total stranger to him; what could she know? One of them was slightly off kilter here, and he knew that he was not the one. He suppressed a sigh, deciding that perhaps those two ladies had been correct in their assessment of the woman. Nevertheless, he forged ahead.

"I'm sorry, but I'm afraid I haven't the vaguest idea what you're talking about." He offered her a sympathetic smile. "You must have mistaken me for someone else."

She shook her head. "No, no mistake about your identity." Her eyes, as green, deep and mystifying as a shaded mountain glen, stared into his. "My mistake was in believing, hoping that by this time you might remember."

"Remember what?" he demanded, his voice rough edged with impatience and a startling deeper sense of disappointment. "I've never seen you before. What's to remember?"

"Oh, lots." The smile she gave him was wistful, overshadowed with longing. "More than you probably could ever imagine."

Adam felt a jolt of something stirring inside his mind, and a thrill of...excitement?...inside his body.

But this was ridiculous, he reasoned, trying and failing to shake off the mental and physical activity. Those two elderly ladies were right; there was something not all together about this woman.

So distracted was he, Adam didn't notice the man coming abreast of them. The soft drawl of the man's voice brought him into awareness.

"Good afternoon, Mistress Dase."

"Good afternoon, sir," she replied respectfully, dipping into a quick curtsy.

Confused by her abrupt change of demeanor, Adam glanced at the man. Obviously another reen-actor, he was elderly, pleasant faced, his costume denoting a personage of means and some standing in the community.

"You are on your way home?" The gentle-man's gaze dropped to the cap dangling from her fingers, then back to her face. A twinkle of intelligent amusement sparkled in his otherwise plain brown eyes.

"Oh…yes." A becoming flush infusing her cheeks, she raised her hands and settled the cap over the knot.

The man's lips twitched. "I wish you a good evening, then," he said, beginning to move on. His laughing eyes made contact with Adam. "And you, also, sir."

"Good evening, sir," she responded.

Thoroughly confused by the exchange, Adam could manage no more than a nod of acknowledgment in return.

"What was that all about?" he asked the moment the gentleman was beyond hearing.

"It's bad form to be out of costume or character while in the area," she answered, an unrepentant smile tugging at her full lips. "He gave me a teasing reminder of my cap."

"I...er..." Adam began, only to be interrupted by the very same gentleman.

"Mistress Dase, on the chance you have forgotten where you are, you are standing in the middle of the road."

She groaned, grabbed Adam's sleeve, and made for the curb before replying, "Ah...yes, thank you, again, sir."

Chuckling, the man went on his way.

The woman beside Adam laughed as well.

Adam shook his head. "I don't understand any of this," he confessed. "Who is that man?"

"A reenactor," she answered, her smile reflecting the laughter lightening her incredible eyes. "This time, his name is Mr. White, and he's playing the role of a very important figure of the period."

Adam's pragmatic mind latched onto two of her words. "This time?" He eyed her warily, as if steeling himself for a sudden flight of fancy. "What do you mean by 'this time'?"

"Oh, he's been here before."

Uh-huh. A wave of regret washed over Adam. The ladies apparently knew whereof they spoke, he thought in abject dejection. Then, gazing at her laughing, beautiful face, another thought sent his spirits soaring on the wings of hope. Perhaps, forewarned and halfway expecting the odd, he had misconstrued her remark. Maybe, just possibly, she had meant that the older gentlemen had done this work before, and at that time had enacted a completely different type of role.

"I see," he said, not quite truthfully. "And... er, have you also done this before?"

"Several times." Her smile shifted from secret delight to soft compassion. "But, of course, you don't remember."

Oh, hell, not again. Adam suppressed a groan, and raked his mind for an intelligent or even merely adequate response, hating the sensation of being way out of his depth. But before he could come up with anything, another, younger voice came into the confusing mix.

"Good afternoon, Mistress Dase."

Turning to the source of the call, Adam observed a young boy loping along on the far side of the street. The bright-faced boy sported a wide grin; his lanky frame was clad in the period clothes of a reenactor.

"Good afternoon, Master Robert," she called, grinning back.

Watching the boy, Adam's mind homed in on one point in particular about the intriguing woman.

"You're name is Daze?"

"Hmm," she murmured, turning to face him.

"Like...in a daze?"

"No." She shook her head. "D-A-S-E." She spelled the name aloud.

"Oh." He frowned, thinking she was as forthcoming as the proverbial clam. "And do you have a first name?"

"Of course. Do you?"

Nudged into remembering common courtesy, he extended his hand. "Adam," he said. "Adam Grainger."

"How do you do, Adam Grainger," she returned in tones of deceptive formality, sliding her hand into his.

The touch of her palm against his, the slight friction of skin on skin, caused an electrifying sensation inside Adam unlike anything he had ever before experienced and way out of proportion to the minimal contact. The thought burst in his mind of what effect he might feel should he touch her lips, her breasts, her...

"Sunshine." Her one spoken word scattered his erotically galloping thoughts.

Adam blinked, then frowned. "What?"

"My given name," she explained.

"Sunshine?" He shook his head—an action he seemed to be repeating frequently since encountering her. "Sunshine Dase?" he asked in patent disbelief. "You're kidding?"

"Nope." Now she shook her head. "That's it."

She grinned. "My parents were repressed flower-children wannabes. But most folks call me Sunny."

Sunny Dase. Oh, Lord. Adam felt torn between a desire to laugh and an urge to groan. "I can't imagine what kind of teasing you must have endured growing up," he murmured in understanding and commiseration.

"It was a challenge," she said, shrugging. "But, as you can see, I survived."

"Very nicely," he commended, skimming a glance over her caped form, feeling his body clench in the process. Nice barely described her appearance, but... Adam wondered if perhaps the trials and tribulations of her former years had been a contributing factor in her strange behavior.

"Thank you, kind sir," she responded, dipping into another quick curtsy. "Actually, I've grown to like the name," she confided. "It's different."

"It is that," he agreed, drolly.

Sunny laughed. And when Sunny laughed like that, easy and spontaneously, the sound literally stole the breath from Adam's body. He had to see her again.

The realization brought sharp awareness of time and place. The late autumn sun was swimming on the horizon, casting a soft golden glow on the surroundings, in the highlights streaking her hair, on her lovely face.

Adam was struck by a sudden overwhelming need to taste the ripe fullness of her lips.

"What are you so deep in thought about?" Sunny's green gaze knowingly probed his eyes, as if reading his mind, discerning his intentions.

Adam had never before met a woman—anyone—with such expressive eyes. The perception in those green depths danced along his nervous system.

Naturally, he couldn't reveal to her what he had been thinking, the desire heating his blood. An eerie intuition telling him she knew the truth of his thoughts, he blurted out, "I was contemplating my chances of success at convincing you to have dinner with me this evening."

"Excellent."

Her prompt response stopped his mental process cold. "Huh?" he said, sounding like a dullard, in all likelihood, because he felt extremely dull and slow-witted. Adam didn't appreciate the feeling. He betrayed himself by stiffening.

Her soft smile smoothed his ruffled feathers. "Your chances of having me accept your invitation to have dinner with you are excellent," she explained.

Astounded by the feelings of elation her acceptance gave him, Adam stared at her a long moment, assimilating the glittering facets of the sensation.

"Where?"

He frowned. "Where what?"

Her laughing eyes mocked him. "Where do you want me to meet you for dinner?" she said precisely.

"Oh. *Oh.*" Adam felt like an idiot, or worse, an awkward hormonally confused teenager. "You don't have to meet me. I'll come for you. If you'll give me directions to..."

"Where are you staying?" she interrupted him to ask, the expression in her eyes softening.

"The Patrick Henry." Adam indicated the upper end of Duke of Gloucester Street with a flick of his hand. "It's across from the restored area, right along Route 60."

"I know where it is." Her expression grew pensive. "Look," she went on after a thoughtful moment, "I'm located close by, right on the fringes of the area. Depending on where you want to have dinner, it would probably be simpler for me to meet you there." She arched her eyebrows. "Did you have a particular place in mind?"

"Well...no," Adam admitted, shrugging. "Actually, although I have made reservations later in the week for several places that were recommended to me by friends, since I only arrived early this afternoon, I was planning to eat at the motel restaurant tonight."

"Then why change your plans?" she said reasonably. "I've eaten there—the food's good. I'll meet you in the lobby at... What time?"

Adam was shaking his head before she'd finished. "Not necessary," he insisted. "I've got a rental car. I can pick you up. It'll be dark. You shouldn't—do not—have to make your own way to the motel."

"I'm a big girl, I can find my way," she said wryly. "It's no hassle for me to hop onto the bus that circles the area. I'll be perfectly safe."

Adam opened his mouth to argue, then immediately shut it again. Her chiding expression said volumes more than her spoken assurances. Advising himself to quit while he was ahead and before she changed her mind, he sighed in defeat.

"Okay, in the lobby at...say, six-thirty?"

"What time is it now?"

He glanced at his watch. "Four thirty-two."

"Suppose we say six," she suggested, her smile enticing. "I haven't eaten since breakfast and I'm famished."

"Six is fine." He offered her a teasing smile. "I'd hate to see you waste away to a shadow of your former self."

"Terrific. See you then." Laughing, she turned away, then slanted a look at him over her shoulder and softly called, "By the way, my *former* self was little more than a shadow."

Not again. A sinking sensation mingling with the anticipation perking inside him, Adam watched her stride away, the long cape swirling around her trim ankles.

Two

"**D**amn."

Washing the trickle of blood from the razor nick on his jaw, Adam dug a styptic pencil out of his shaving kit and grimaced as he applied it to the minor wound. The grimace wasn't in reaction to the sting of the pencil, but to the visible tremor in his fingers.

Ridiculous, Adam decided, flinging the towel aside and striding into the bedroom.

He was always cool, collected and logical. He ran a far-ranging family-owned corporation. He never lost his composure, maintaining his vaunted, steel-edged control through even the most intensely fought business battles.

The very idea of him suffering so much as a slight case of the shakes over the prospect of spending time with a woman was a concept beyond the pale.

Ms. Sunny Dase—preposterous name!—intrigued him, Adam concluded, absently rejecting one shirt in favor of another, too distracted to take note of his unusual indecisiveness concerning his choice of apparel.

Every article of clothing Adam possessed was well made, elegant, tasteful and outrageously expensive. Whatever he chose to wear suited him and any occasion. Formal wear excepted.

Should he wear a tie—or go for a more casual look?

The thought jolted Adam into the realization that he was actually agonizing over a necktie.

Was he losing his mind...or simply bewitched?

The follow-up thought brought a wry smile to his compressed lips. The consideration of bewitchment immediately wiped the smile from his mouth.

Nonsense.

Sunny was an enigma, a puzzle, nothing more. Adam had earned a reputation for his ability to untangle puzzles and expose supposed enigmas.

But she did possess the power to excite him. He had felt the zing and sting of that power with his first sight of her striding across the Palace Green.

Forgoing the neck wear, Adam felt a recurring sizzle dance along his nerve endings as he shrugged into his jacket. He would be meeting Sunny in exactly...

He shot a glance at his wristwatch. Another jolt went through him. While he had been musing on his limited sartorial section, time had slipped away from him.

Scooping his loose change, wallet and keys from atop the dresser, he shoved them into his pockets as he strode into the sitting room of the suite, then to the door. He had never known a woman to be on time. Still, he had three and a half minutes to get his rump down to the lobby—in the unlikely event Sunny proved to be the exception.

She was waiting for him.

The sight of her, standing at ease and relaxed next to the impressive bust of Patrick Henry on a pedestal in the lobby, not only surprised but delighted Adam.

The contrast in her attire alone was startling. Whereas before she had appeared the picture of an eighteenth-century maiden in her period costume, with her hair pulled up into a loose knot on top of her head, Sunny now projected an image of an ultramodern, thoroughly ''with it'' young woman.

She was dressed in a severely cut, perfectly fit, austere-looking black suit, with a figure-hugging pencil-slim ankle-length skirt, the side seems slit to just above the knees. The peek of curvaceous calves, in addition to her enticingly rounded bottom and long, slender thighs, caused a sudden dry tightness in Adam's throat.

Swallowing with some difficulty, he shifted his gaze, giving her person a more encompassing look.

The severity of her black suit was balanced by a snowy white blouse with a froth of lace at the collar and cuffs, the lace spilling over the backs of her hands. Sheer black nylon encased her legs. Her slim, delicate feet were enhanced by high-heeled black suede evening pumps.

Slowly, reluctantly, Adam dragged his gaze up along the alluring lines of her body and settled on her face. She appeared to be wearing a minimum of makeup: perhaps a light, translucent base, a brush of color on her cheeks; a darkening swish of mascara on her lashes; a clear, true red applied to her luscious lips.

Gliding his tongue over his own lips, Adam forced his glance away from temptation, past her straight nose, the glowing skin of her cheeks, the alert and bright interest in her curious green eyes, to the top of her head and...

And her hair... Oh, Lord, her hair. Sunny's wavy mane of gold-streaked brown hair tumbled onto her shoulders and halfway down her elegantly straight spine.

In truth, the sight of her took his breath away. Adam's fingers twitched with the desire to spear into the alluring brown mass; his mind reeled with an image of those gold-streaked strands spread out on a pillow...his pillow.

But first things first, he advised himself, crossing the lobby to her. Dinner, then...

"Hello," he said, attempting to corral his bed-bent thoughts as he came to a halt beside her. "Were you early or am I late?"

"Oh...hi." Sunny flashed a nerve-crunching smile at him. "Since it is now precisely six, you are not late. So I guess I was a few moments early. No big deal."

"Even so, I'm sorry I kept you waiting." Adam replied, appalled by the slight catch in his voice, the rapid beat of his heart, the quivery sensation inside him...all direct effects of her disarming smile.

Boy, he mused, inwardly shaken by his response, mentally and physically. He had heard about dynamite smiles, had even witnessed a few, but this woman's smile went way beyond dynamite; megaton came closer to the mark.

"Still hungry?" he asked politely, quashing a different hunger expanding inside.

"Starved." Though her tone was somber, her eyes, those amazingly expressive green eyes, conveyed her understanding of and amusement at his unstated appetite.

Batten down the hatches, Mabel, there's a rock-a-butzer storm gathering on the horizon.

The sudden recollection of one of Adam's late

father's favorite expressions in times of trouble had a settling effect on his equilibrium, easing the strain from his voice, allowing him to return her perceptive smile.

"In that case, I suppose I'd better feed you." Taking her by the hand, Adam steered her to the restaurant.

"My hero," Sunny murmured, batting her eyelashes—her long, dark eyelashes—at him. Then, as she moved around the bust, she drew her fingers along the chiseled jawline of Patrick Henry. "It's a good likeness," she said, slanting a teasing look at him. "The fiery radical would be pleased."

Adam laughed at her whimsy, but composed himself enough to give his name to the pleasant-faced hostess standing in the restaurant entrance, checking names against the leather-bound reservation list in her hands.

"Ah, yes, good evening, Mr. Grainger." She offered a smile and an ushering movement of her hand. "Right this way. Your table is ready."

"Have you eaten here before?" Sunny asked, after they were seated and proffered menus, when the hostess had departed.

Adam shook his head. "No. I didn't get in until early this afternoon. I had lunch on the plane." He grinned. "Unlike some, I find nothing wrong with the in-flight food. In truth, I thoroughly enjoy it."

"So do I." She grinned back at him. "Does that make us peasants or merely plebeian?"

"Or, just maybe, it makes us too honest to affect a pseudosophistication," he suggested.

"Yes," she agreed, giving him the chills with the soft look she swept over him. "You always were...honest, I mean, almost to a fault."

Not again, Adam thought, smothering a groan. Not yet another not-too-veiled reference to them having met, known each other before.

Still, he couldn't deny the spark of interest her remark generated.

Studying her, and more than a little impressed by her clear-eyed and direct regard in return, Adam decided that perhaps it was time he probed the depths of her assumed previous knowledge of him, his personality.

"We've only just met," he said. "How could you possibly know that I've always been honest."

Her eyes darkened, as if with an inner amused knowing. A gently mocking smile kissed her lips, making his mouth ache with desire to do likewise.

"I've known almost forever."

"Indeed?" The skeptical arch of one eyebrow underscored his tone of voice.

"Yes." Though quiet, her tone was absolute.

"But, how?" he persisted. "How could..."

Adam broke off with the arrival of a waiter at the table. He concealed his impatience until they had given their drink and dinner orders and the man had left them.

"How?" he repeated the moment they were

alone again. "How could you know anything about me?"

"Oh, Andrew…"

"Adam," he interjected, his voice taut and impatient. "My name is Adam."

"Of course." She winced. "I'm sorry." The expression in her eyes revealed the depth of her contrition. "I…I'm having some difficulty keeping the two separated."

Adam was struck by a blast of feeling, too close to jealously to be acceptable. Dammit, he thought, he barely knew the woman. How could he be jealous?

"We are so alike, this Andrew and I?" he asked, in a harsh tone made almost cruel by his inner struggle of denial.

"Yes." A gentle smile curved her lips. "But please try to understand, you are alike because you are one, the same being, the same soul."

Oh, hell. A New Age basket case.

Adam wasn't into New Age. He was too busy staying on the cutting edge of his current age.

Disappointment bruised his mind. Sunny had caught Adam's interest from his first sight of her. She was not only lovely but fascinating, exciting, different. Too different.

"You're having trouble dealing with this." Her voice was soft, her tone sympathetic.

Staring at her, at the concerned expression dimming the glow in her fantastic eyes, Adam was only vaguely aware of the waiter silently placing their drinks in front of them, then moving away again.

"Have a sip of your wine. It might help a little," she suggested.

Distracted, Adam picked up the stemmed goblet, took a generous swallow of the dark red wine, then frowned. Why had he ordered it? Other than for toasting purposes on holidays, birthday gatherings, weddings and such, he didn't drink wine, preferring light beer, or when in need of fortification and something stronger, bourbon or scotch, neat.

He transferred his frown to Sunny. "Did I order this—what is it, anyway? Burgundy?" It was a pure guess.

"Yes." The glow flared to life again in her eyes. "And yes, you did order it."

"Odd."

"Not to me," she said, her smile nostalgic. "It was always your wine of preference...even with a fish or fowl course."

Adam felt his facial muscles tighten and his stomach clench. "Don't start that *always* business again. I'm not buying into it."

"You will...eventually." Once more, her smile and the glow in her eyes faded. "At least, I pray you will."

This was getting heavy, Adam told himself. And he was getting edgy.

"Look, Sunny," he began, determined to stay calm and reasonable. "I'm not sure..." he broke off as the waiter put in another appearance at the table, this time to deliver their soup course.

After smiling and thanking the waiter, Sunny glanced down at the creamy potato-leek soup the man had set before her, then back up at Adam.

"Could we postpone further discussion until after we've eaten?" she asked. "I truly am very hungry."

It wasn't easy, but drawing a deep breath, Adam managed to temper his impatience. Besides, he was hungry, too, and the soup did look inviting.

"Okay." He watched her take a sample taste of her soup; his breath got stuck in his throat as her lips closed around the bowl of the spoon. "Good?" he asked, despairing of the dry catch in his voice.

"Mmm," Sunny nodded, dipping the spoon into the creamy broth once again. "Heavenly."

"You're right," he murmured, after his first sip. "Absolutely heavenly."

Though she smiled, she made no response.

Adam concluded that when the hungry Sunny involved herself with eating, her involvement was complete. He couldn't help but wonder if she became as deeply involved while in the process of assuaging a different, more earthy appetite.

The soup was consumed in silence. While polishing off his soup, Adam was consumed by erotic images of Sunny, feasting on the sustenance of his mouth.

"Oh, that was wonderful," she said when the last drop had been scooped from the bowl. She grinned. "Had I known, I wouldn't have had to order the salmon. I could have made a meal of a large bowl of the soup."

I could make a meal of you.

The smile that tugged at Adam's lips was more in response to his thought than Sunny's impish grin.

"We could change your..." he began, then shook his head on sight of the waiter approaching the table, a large tray balanced on one palm and held aloft at shoulder level. "No, we couldn't," he went on, lowering his voice as the waiter came to a stop. "You'll have to settle for the fish."

"Oh, that's okay." She shrugged. "I like fish...as you should know."

Adam scowled at her and at the taunting remark and undertones of her voice.

Of course, with the waiter there, he could not retaliate or even question her assertion, not without sounding like a reject from a New Age publishing house.

"Mmm, it all looks and smells delicious." Sunny gave the waiter a decidedly sunny smile. "Thank you."

"You're welcome," he replied, returning her smile full wattage, while sparing a mere glance at

Adam. "Ma'am, sir, enjoy your dinner." Giving a half bow from the waist, he withdrew from the table.

"Nice young man, isn't he?" she asked, brightly.

"Charming," he said, darkly.

Her lips twitched; her eyes teased. "I do love the sound of that gentle Virginia drawl."

Adam grunted and slanted a pointed look at her plate. "I thought you were starving?"

"That was before the soup," she said, pleasantly. "Now I'm merely hungry."

"Then eat." Adam was chagrined by the snarling sound of his voice, and even more so by the startling rush of emotions that had caused it.

That old green-eyed monster again?

First that gut-wrenching twinge because he thought Sunny's reference to an Andrew was to an actual, living, breathing man, and now because of a pleasant, soft-spoken—incidentally good looking—young waiter?

Adam rejected the very idea; or at least he tried to reject it. Problem was, it wouldn't stay rejected. His mind persisted in examining the phenomenon.

Could he actually be jealous of the smile, the brief attention she had bestowed upon the seemingly ubiquitous waiter? he mused uncomfortably.

Ridiculous. He barely knew the woman—and he wasn't too sure about her mental stability. The very idea of him being jealous was ludicrous in the extreme.

So why, then, was he feeling as if he wanted to break things, starting with the Virginia drawl-voiced waiter?

"Have you lost your appetite?"

Sunny's question intruded upon his unappealing ruminations. For the salmon in dill sauce, yes, he answered in silent frustration. But for her, dammit, no.

Noting with some surprise that she had made inroads into her meal, Adam avoided responding by posing a query of his own. "Is it good?"

"Excellent." She smiled; his pulses raced. "But why not try it for yourself?"

He did. She was right. It was excellent. But Adam was no longer hungry. Not for food. Nevertheless, he continued to eat, growing more restless by the minute.

When at last they had finished and the charming waiter had served their coffee and removed their plates and himself, Adam determined to have answers.

"Okay, you said you'd explain after dinner." He arched his eyebrows. "I'm listening."

Sunny gnawed on her lip and glanced around at the laughing, chatting diners crowding the room. "Not here," she murmured. "I'd prefer somewhere more private."

"Like one of the seating areas in the lobby?"

"Or, better yet... Perhaps, your room?"

Three

Sunny's prosaically delivered suggestion had an electrifying effect on Adam.

Did she realize the connotations he could...*was* attaching to her proposal? he reflected, staring at her expectant expression in surprised disbelief. Or, he further mused, had she tossed out a deliberate proposition?

The concept didn't seem to fit what Adam had thus far garnered about her character—but on the other hand, what he actually knew about Miss Sunshine Dase was in fact sorely lacking in evidence.

"Of course, if you prefer one of the seating areas..." she said, shrugging when his silence lengthened.

"Not at all," Adam was quick to assure her, taking a deep swallow of his coffee in hopes of relieving the sudden dryness in his throat. "You just caught me off guard," he admitted, draining the cup before continuing, "I...er, you're not afraid or even uncertain of being alone with me?"

"Not at all," Sunny mimicked, softening her gentle mockery with a confident smile. "I have never, would never, will never be afraid or uncertain of being alone with you."

"Why not?" he asked at once, his voice harsh with demand. "What assurance do you have?"

"Because I know you...so well." Her voice held a note of wistfulness, her eyes, those deep green windows to her soul, were shadowed with regret. "I know you would sacrifice yourself before you would deliberately hurt me."

Oh, God. What had he gotten into here? Adam asked himself, feeling torn between conflicting, yet equal desires. While part of him, the down-to-earth, logical part, urged him to retreat, another part, the captivated, fascinated part, demanded he forge ahead, explore the possibilities.

The inner conflict must have been written plain as day in his expression; it became obvious that Sunny had no difficulty reading him like an open book.

"You can always change your mind," she offered, keeping her expression devoid of whatever she might be feeling.

"No." The instant decision made and voiced, Adam placed his napkin on the table. "I'm ready whenever you are."

Sunny didn't respond verbally; she made her intent clear by mirroring his act of discarding her napkin.

After signing the check and tipping the waiter, Adam escorted Sunny from the restaurant and directly to the elevators.

In a silence fraught with questions, doubts and a building desire he could not deny, Adam stood beside her during the brief ascent to his floor and walked beside her along the hallway to his suite.

Tension crawled along his nervous system as he pulled shut the door behind them, enclosing them in privacy. A wry smile touched his lips at the thought that at least the bed wasn't the first thing they saw on entering the sitting room.

"Very nice," she murmured, glancing around the room before raising teasing eyes to his. "Do you always take a suite of rooms when you travel?"

"No." Adam shook his head. "I usually don't spend enough time in the room to care, either way. I took this suite simply because it was all that was available." He flicked a hand to indicate the cozy grouping of settee and two chairs. "Make yourself comfortable."

"In a moment," she said, tossing her cape over the back of a chair as she crossed to the wide window, framed by the open drapes. "The pool area looks rather desolate," she observed, turning her head to smile at him. "Doesn't it?"

"Yeah," he agreed, wondering how much time she would waste on small-talk inanities before getting around to meaningful explanations. "But, then, despite the mild weather, it is December, isn't it?"

"Yes." She turned her back on the window, as if dismissing the scene beyond the pane. "Less than two weeks to go until Christmas."

"Hmm." Adam nodded; one subject closed. "May I get you a drink? There's a good selection in the mini bar."

Sunny started to shake her head no, then appeared to change her mind. "Yes, why not. I have a lot to tell you. It'll keep my throat moist. I'll have the white wine..." She paused to smile. "You may have the red."

So, she wasn't planning to procrastinate, he thought, going to the small drinks cabinet while Sunny settled into one corner of the settee. Breaking the seal, he unlocked the cabinet, removed two small bottles, then emptied the contents into the stemmed glasses set on a tray atop the cabinet.

After handing one of the glasses to her, he settled into the other corner of the settee.

The way Sunny sat, knees together, legs turned into the settee, gave him a tantalizing view of her shapely calves and trim ankles, revealed by the gap in her side-slit skirt. The sight both excited and amused Adam. Here he was, unbelievably turned on by the everyday look of a woman's legs below the knee. Incredible.

"Your health," he murmured. Suddenly very thirsty, he raised the glass to her before bringing it to his lips to sample the dark red liquid.

"And yours," she said, following his example.

Adam was barely aware of her response; he was too distracted by the sudden realization of having chosen the wine, a cabernet this time, instead of his normally preferred can of light beer.

Weird. And yet...

The astounding thing was, he found himself savoring the rich, full-bodied flavor of the wine.

Weird, indeed. But then, weird seemed par for the course ever since his first encounter with Sunny, when she had appeared to recognize him and called him Andrew.

Sunny took a sip of her wine, then glided the tip of her tongue over her upper lip.

A deliberate, seductive maneuver? Adam wondered. A flickering coil of heat in the foundation of his manhood gave ample evidence that if it was a deliberate ploy, it had definitely succeeded. He was experiencing the discomfort to prove it.

"Before I begin," she began, "I would like you to answer a question for me."

What game was she playing, anyway? Adam

took another swallow of his wine to conceal his cynical smile.

Nevertheless, cynicism or not, he decided to play along with her—for the moment.

"Ask anything you like," he invited expansively. "*I* have nothing to hide."

If Sunny noticed the emphasis he'd placed on the "I," she chose to ignore it.

"From your mention of friends having recommended restaurants to you and your reaction to the wagon on the street earlier, I presume that this is your first visit to the restored area of Colonial Williamsburg." She raised her delicately arched eyebrows. "Am I correct?"

"Yes." He frowned. "Why?"

"And..." She smiled. "You're obviously alone."

"Yes." His frown deepened. "Why?"

"That's what I'm getting at."

"Excuse me?" Adam made a production of exhaling. "I'm afraid I missed something. You want to back that up and run it by me again?"

"You are here alone."

Impatience scraped against Adam's nerves. "I thought I had made that clear." His voice and the muscles in his jaw were tight. "Yes, I am alone."

"Why?"

When had their roles switched? Adam asked himself, striving to hang on to control. When had

Sunny become the interrogator and he the inter-
rogatee?

"Why am I alone?" His voice had a grating
edge.

"Why are you here…alone." Sunny gave a
quick impatient shake of her head. "Why did you
come here alone?"

Good question, Adam conceded. Too bad he
didn't have a good answer. He pondered a response for a moment, then with a mental shrug,
decided to go with the unvarnished truth, odd as
it might sound.

"Believe it or not, I'm here, at this family time
of year, because of a whim."

"A whim," she repeated, her wry tone giving
evidence of disbelief. "Of course."

"A whim," he repeated, adamantly.

"You have no family?"

"Yes, I have family," he answered. "Two
brothers and a sister, all younger and all unmar-
ried…" He paused a beat before adding, "As I
am."

"No wife or significant other?"

"No wife or significant other," he echoed, gri-
macing at the current term for girlfriend or lover.
He hesitated, almost afraid to ask the next logical
question, yet aware he had to know the answer.
"Do you have family somewhere, your parents,
siblings…a husband?"

"Parents, yes, and a brother and sister, both

older, both married, with one child apiece, all living in northern California.''

"No husband?" He arched his brows. "Or significant other in your life?''

"No.''

"Why?''

"I could ask the same of you.'' Her eyebrows rose in reflection of his.

Adam felt caught in a trap of his own devising. He didn't want to answer, resisted the self exposure of explaining his reluctance to commit to any one woman. And yet, he wanted to hear her reasons for remaining single.

Sunny waited in calm patience for him to respond, as if she somehow knew the inner struggle he was waging. To Adam's way of thinking, her apparent *knowing* was more than unnerving, it was damn creepy.

She raised her glass and sipped at the wine, all the while maintaining eye contact with him.

Adam smiled, conceding victory to her in the silent war of wills. "I have just never found a woman with whom I wanted to share either my life or my space,'' he said, hoping the explanation was enough to satisfy her. He should have known better, even after such a short acquaintance.

"Found?'' Sunny pounced on the word. "Found presupposes that you've been looking.''

"Not actively,'' he hedged. "Have you?'' he shot back. "Been looking, I mean?''

"Actively," she admitted. "For you."

Adam heaved a long-suffering sigh. "Why do I have this feeling I've landed in the middle of a particularly weird episode of 'The Twilight Zone'?" he asked, as much of himself as of her.

She laughed. "Scary, huh?"

"More like dumb," he retaliated.

"Perhaps." She shrugged. "Nevertheless, for certain reasons we are both unattached."

Adam slowly expelled another heartfelt sight. "So, you're basically alone here."

"Yes. My choice." She smiled. "And you are here, now, in reaction to a whim."

Adam suddenly felt funny—funny odd, not funny ha-ha. He didn't like the feeling, and so felt compelled to explain, which wasn't easy since he wasn't accustomed to explaining his motives or actions to anyone and since he wasn't certain he himself understood the whim, or impulse, or whatever.

"A couple of weeks ago, I turned on the TV to catch the news," he began, hoping to discern some sense of it for himself while explaining to her. "As a rule, I watch little television, but, since I head up the family owned business, I do like to stay abreast of what's going on in the business world."

"You're the CEO?"

"Yes—" he smiled "—which only means I ride herd over the other members of my family." Then he laughed aloud. "We're a diverse and far-flung bunch, one running a casino in Deadwood, one managing a ranch in Montana, the youngest doing her fashion thing in San Francisco. And then there are other interests, oil, computer software,'' he went on, wondering why in the hell he was babbling away to her, when he was usually closed-mouth. And yet, his smile wry, he continued on, just the same.

"It's a tough job but somebody has to do it. Since I'm the eldest of the lot, I inherited the job of holding the corporate strings and keeping them from tangling.''

"And I suspect you do it very well,'' she murmured.

He shrugged. "There have been no complaints...so far.'' Frowning at his sudden propensity to shoot his mouth off, Adam brought himself back to the point of discussion. "At any rate, I was in front of the TV. During a break, a commercial came on extolling the attractions of Colonial Williamsburg at Christmastime.'' He gave a half laugh, half snort. "I wasn't even paying attention...and yet...''

"You felt drawn,'' she murmured into the quiet space left by his voice trailing off.

"Yes.'' Adam cringed inwardly at the detectable strain in his voice.

"Yes.'' The understanding in her eyes reflected her solemn tone. "I know.''

"How do you know?" he demanded, the strain in his voice rough edged.

"I've felt it, that compelling draw," she replied, her voice a bare whisper. "Many times."

"I don't understand any of this." Gulping down the last of the wine, Adam rose and went to the drinks cabinet to withdraw another small bottle. "Are you ready for another?" he asked, in a near snarl.

"No." Sunny shook her head, setting her hair rippling against her shoulders and back.

Adam shuddered in response to the sight of the long, swirling strands, the gold highlights glinting in the glow from the table lamps. His hands ached to bury themselves in the silken mass. In reflex, his fingers clenched around the delicate stem of the wineglass.

"You're angry," she murmured, staring pointedly at his white-knuckled grip.

And aroused, he replied in silent frustration, glaring at the offending digits. When had he ever responded to a woman—any woman—like this? Never. Adam knew full well that he had never before in his life, not even as a young and admittedly horny man reacted so strongly to a woman.

"Adam."

"What?" Startled by the harsh sound of his own voice, he sliced a quick, hard look at her.

"Come sit down, please." She drew a slow

breath, then went on, "I have a story…several stories, to tell you."

Recalling the tales of Scheherazade, Adam smiled, wryly, took a fortifying swallow of his wine, and returned to settle again on the opposite corner of the settee.

"About what?" He raised his brows in a deliberate arch of skepticism.

"Seasons past," she answered, her beautiful, revealing eyes filled with gut-wrenching sadness.

Shifting mental gears away from the tales of Scheherazade, Adam suddenly recalled another tale and the visit of Dickens's fictional ghost to Scrooge. Smiling in an attempt to ease the tension in the muscles banding his stomach, he repeated the miser's response to the specter.

"Long past?"

Sunny's return smile was soft, melancholic.

"Our past."

Adam had reached the point of explosion. Leaping to his feet and nearly spilling the wine in the process, he took the two steps necessary to close the distance between them. Bending down, he brought his face to within inches of hers.

"Dammit, woman," he erupted. "We have no past. I never laid eyes on you before this afternoon." Even as he made the claim, Adam felt a twinge of conscience, recollecting the shock of recognition he'd experienced earlier as she had come abreast of him in the street.

Nevertheless, he asserted, "I have never met you, don't know you and you sure as hell can't know me."

"Oh, but I do," Sunny persisted, accepting his narrow-eyed glare with fearless composure. "I would know you anywhere, in any setting."

Though he was loath to admit it, Adam was impressed by her steady regard, her calm voice. An uneasiness crawling through him, he straightened and stepped back.

"How do you know me?" he muttered, unconscious of appearing to retreat as he took another step back and resumed his seat on the corner of the settee. "How...when we have never met, never seen each other?"

"Not in this lifetime, no," she agreed.

Oh, hell, he thought savagely, seeing his hopes of a mutually satisfying holiday dalliance growing dimmer with each adamant new statement she made. Dejection weighed heavy on him at the realization that he, a man noted for his scrupulous selectivity in regards to female companionship, now found himself attracted—strongly attracted—to a blazing New Age cuckoo bird. The Twilight Zone indeed.

It was pretty damned depressing.

"Other than a few subtle differences, your appearance has always been basically the same."

Sunny's quiet voiced observation jolted Adam from the depths of introspection.

"No kidding." His voice was threaded with sarcasm and cynicism.

"No kidding." Her voice was soft, tender with understanding and compassion.

Adam groaned.

Sunny smiled. Her eyes, those all-knowing fantastic green pools of enticement, began a slow, careful inventory of his physical features.

"You were ever a handsome man."

Adam felt both thrilled and shaken by her prosaically voiced remark, the absolute belief in her tone. While he was delighted she found him attractive, he was equally dismayed by her phrasing.

"Ever?" he repeated the word that bothered him.

"Yes." Her unhurried gaze traced the bone structure of his face. "Broad forehead, dark brows winged over deep-set, deeply intelligent indigo-blue eyes."

A ripple of something crept through Adam, but he wasn't given time to examine that something, for her gaze and commentary moved on.

"High cheekbones, long, straight nose jutting above a sculpted mouth, the upper lip thin, imperious, the lower lip fuller, sensuous, the face resting upon a rock-solid, squarely chiseled jawline, the whole crowned by a thick and silky mane of auburn waves."

Adam would have laughed, ridiculed, had he been able to force sound from his amazement-parched throat. But it didn't matter, Sunny didn't wait for a response. She continued on, her gaze moving lower.

"A strong neck column supporting the head, with wide, muscular shoulders supporting the column. Broad chest, not deep but flatly muscled—" she smiled "—with, I suspect, a matting thatch of soft auburn curls, the hair narrowing from the diamond shape, arrowing down the center of the torso."

Adam swallowed, opened his mouth, then swallowed again. How could she know, be so certain? he wondered, the uneasiness mixing with an expanding excitement inside him. Not all men were the same; some had chests that were practically hairless, while others were furred all over. How could Sunny know, so correctly describe his chest?

"Slim waist, narrow hips, flat, almost concave abdomen." Once again, her soft voice snagged his attention. "Long, straight legs, the thighs and calves tightly muscled. And supporting the entirety of the over-six-foot frame, big, solid feet…"

Sunny paused an instant, her eyebrows arching over eyes laughing into his. "Reflecting another, more sensitive and delicate attribute?"

Adam could barely think, barely breathe, never mind attempt to speak. A sense of near fright gripped his mind, while sheer sexual excitement held his body in thrall, pulsating to the cadence of her soft voice.

"And inside, where you live, I suspect you're the same, as well," she continued, her voice lower, gentle, but rock solid in conviction.

"Meaning?" Adam asked, his voice barely there, but needing to hear the answer.

She smiled. "You are mentally strong, self-confident, honest and honorable. You are equally strong physically, with a healthy degree of sensuality, tempered by a personal sense of fastidiousness."

How could she know? he wondered, raking his mind for a logical explanation that eluded him.

Damn. Damn. How the hell could she know?

Four

"You're finding this, all of this, difficult to deal with. Aren't you?"

Adam laughed; the harsh sound grated on his ears. "Oh, yeah," he drawled, not at all convincingly. "I'm finding it difficult." He grimaced. "In actual truth, I'm finding it—you—a tad more than bizarre."

"Of course."

Her calm acceptance was the last straw.

"What the hell do you mean, of course?" he snapped. "None of what you said makes any sense, and your only comment is 'of course'?" He gave a sharp shake of his head. "You're going to have to do better than that, Ms. Sunshine Dase. A whole helluva lot better."

"I know." Sunny took a quick sip of wine, then ran her tongue over her lips, sending a shiver down the length of Adam's spine. "And I will."

Adam made a show of glancing at his watch. "It's already after eight," he said, his tone deliberately sardonic. "Were you planning to begin any time soon?"

"There was one particularly glorious spring."

Adam frowned. "I beg your pardon?"

"You asked me to begin." She smiled. "And I have. But if you intend to continue interrupting..." She let her voice fade, and raised her eyebrows.

"Okay, I got the message." Adam sighed, loudly. "Please do go on—I'll keep my mouth shut."

Sunny's lips twitched, but she managed to contain her obvious desire to laugh...at him.

"As I was saying," she said, silent laughter skipping along her voice. "There was one particular spring. In Britannia. I believe it was during the first century, when the Roman legions conquered the Celtic tribes."

"What?" Adam actually jolted in shock.

"Well, I'm not quite sure of the exact date." She lifted her shoulders in a helpless half shrug. "That part's a little cloudy. But I do know it was during the Roman occupation of the British Isles," she explained brightly.

Adam eyed her suspiciously. Either she was giving a good yank on his leg or she was a functioning nut case. He wasn't well pleased with either possibility.

"You're putting me on...right?"

"No." She shook her head. "That is the first memory I have of us together, and it's fuzzy around the edges."

"Memory?" Adam was beginning to feel like a parrot, which was bad enough. But even worse, he was beginning to feel uncomfortably like a fool, a dupe, and that feeling could hardly be borne. He had never been anyone's fool or dupe, and he wasn't planning on starting with Sunny. However, he was curious about her purpose, what end she hoped to achieve with the line she was unreeling.

"Yes, memory," she said. "The first one of many memories, of you and me, of tragedy and love."

"Sounds like a pop-song title," he murmured in droll tones. "But do go on."

"I know it's hard to believe..."

Try impossible, he thought, squashing the impulse to interrupt by voicing the observation.

"I had a great deal of trouble with it myself at the beginning." A shadow darkened her eyes, turning them to a shade of deep forest green.

Fighting a sudden longing to get lost in that forest, Adam's voice came out rough edged. "And when was that?"

"When I was still too young to understand,"

Sunny explained, her smile wistful for the child she had been. "I never told anyone then about them...the scenes that without warning flashed through my mind. There were just bits and pieces, really only fragments of scenes. But as I grew older, into my teens, they got stronger, more expanded, vivid with the color and action of life and death and love." Her voice, so low, intense, caused a shiver to raise the hairs on Adam's arms. "Love gained and love lost and love forever."

When she paused to take a sip of wine, Adam wanted to laugh in her face, tell her to take a hike and take her loopy stories with her. He wanted to, but he couldn't. He felt strangely breathless, caught by the obvious tension gripping her, the almost otherworldly quality of her voice.

He tried to speak, cleared his voice, but by then it was too late: Sunny resumed her narrative.

"Although in some respects, exact chronological time and place, the scenes were still fuzzy, particular aspects were clear and sharp." Her faraway gaze sketched his features. "You were there, not as a druid or learned man but a warrior, straight and tall, breathtakingly handsome even in blue paint, a true Celt, your below shoulder-length dark hair gleaming auburn in the sunlight, your magnificent physical power fierce but never savage."

Adam felt rather savage at that moment—or was it savaged? he mused, unsettled by her description of him, a description, moreover, that still fit him—in certain respects.

"You haven't changed much, have you?" Sunny asked, her eyes alight with humor.

He scowled.

She laughed. "Oh, as the old advertisement claimed, You've come a long way, baby," she said. "But basically you've maintained the same strong, fierce personality." She smiled. "You are simply fighting a different kind of war, with the boardroom as your battlefield."

Could she read minds? Adam wondered, his gaze narrow and intent on her smiling face. Although he didn't believe in the possibility of ESP and the like, the consideration gave him pause, because, if she could somehow discern his thoughts, she would know how very tempted he was to kiss her smiling mouth, test the softness of her lips, taste the sweetness within, plunge his tongue into her honey.

"What are you thinking?" Sunny eyed him with undisguised suspicion.

Adam couldn't suppress a chuckle, or the impulse to answer with the unvarnished truth.

"I'm thinking about how badly I want to kiss you," he admitted. "For starters."

He didn't know what to expect in a response from her. Still, he was pleasantly surprised when she grinned.

"It's nice to know that along with your strength you've retained your sensuous hunger."

"And you've...er, enjoyed that before?" Adam asked, astounded at himself for doing so, as if he were actually starting to believe her incredulous revelations.

"Enjoyed it?" Sunny's voice was soft, low, throaty and electrifyingly exciting. "I reveled in the pure pleasure of it...and you."

"A lotus-eater, hmm?" He arched a teasing brow, while tamping the urge to grab her, drag her across the twelve or so inches separating them, and crush her mouth and her body with his own.

"Among other things."

That did it. Her assertion, and the smoky expression in her slumberous eyes, broke the control Adam was exerting over his natural impulses. Moving with slow deliberation, he set his glass aside. A sizzle shot through him, straight to the heat of him, when she followed his example.

He moved toward her.

Sunny moved toward him.

They met in the center of the settee.

"I'm going to kiss you," he said in warning.

"I sincerely hope so," she said in encouragement.

And then he had her in his arms, arms—he noticed in amazement—that trembled, in much the same way her lips trembled in anticipation.

Staring into Sunny's eyes, losing his sense and

senses in their beckoning green depths, Adam slowly lowered his head to her raised face.

Her lips parted.

He felt the breath of her sigh as he covered her mouth with his own.

The taste of her was ambrosia, every bit as sweet as he had thought she would be. Deepening the kiss, Adam slid his hands up her spine to tangle his fingers in the silken mass of her hair. The effect on his senses was immediate, hot and exciting; like touching sunbaked satin.

He made a tentative foray with his tongue, lightly skimming the tender inner skin of her lower lip. She responded with a low moan, which sounded to him like *more.*

Emboldened, Adam slipped his tongue between her lips. Heaven, a haven, not a place to visit. A home. A place to stay, longed for, never fully forgotten.

Home? Never forgotten. What in the world?

Unnerved by the sudden vague and confusing thought, he pulled back, releasing his hold on her mouth and her quivering body, putting inches of breathing space between them.

Sunny stared at him from passion-shadowed eyes, her breathing betrayingly quick and erratic.

Damning his own need to gasp for breath, his desire to pull her back into his embrace, Adam steeled himself against the silent plea in her eyes.

"This is crazy."

"What is?" she asked, her voice strained and unsteady. "The sexual attraction you're feeling for a virtual stranger? Or the comfort of familiarity you experienced with that sexual attraction?"

How in the hell does she know?

"This whole situation is crazy," he snapped, avoiding a direct answer to her question. "I've had some easy conquests, but never anything as quick and easy as this."

"It was always easy for you to conquer... antagonists, nature and women."

"Really?" Suspicion tinged his tone. "What are you after?"

"You."

Sunny's simply stated response shot steel into his spine, among other things. Ignoring the physical discomfort, he concentrated on the fuller meaning of her reply.

"Why?"

"Because you promised."

"What?" Adam shook his head, wondering if he had missed something or if he was losing it.

"I said, because you promised."

"I heard you." Afraid that he really might be losing it, Adam controlled an urge to shout. "What I want to hear is an explanation, because I never promised you a thing."

Sunny sighed. "I guess I'd better return to my story, and I'd appreciate it if you didn't interrupt this time."

"Have at it," he invited, giving an expansive wave of his hand, which he was far from feeling.

"Thank you." She began a smile that dissolved into a frown of consternation. "Where was I?"

"In Brittania," he said with gritty sarcasm. "With the Romans and the blue-painted Celts."

"Yes...the Celts." Her smile held a puzzled quality. "It was odd, but as I grew out of my teens and the flashing memories intensified, I began to understand what the voices were saying, even though the language was unintelligible to me, sounding archaic."

"Voices?" Adam said, reneging on his agreement not to interrupt. "You heard voices?"

"Well, of course." Sunny frowned. "The scenes I viewed inside my head were quite like brief individual frames from a roll of film."

"Complete with wraparound sound, I presume?" His attempt at inserting a dash of humor into her story concoction fell upon deaf ears.

"Exactly!" Sunny beamed at him in approval.

"I see." Adam suppressed a sigh. "Do go on." In truth, he could hardly wait to hear more—although the threat of dire results couldn't have made him admit to the anticipation he felt. "You understood the voices."

"Yes." She frowned. "I don't know how, but I simply knew what they were saying."

"They?" He played the echo once again.

"The people in the images," she clarified. "At

first they frightened me." She smiled. "They were so…" She hesitated, as if searching for the right description. "They were all so different, fierce and almost wild in appearance. Not at all like the humans I was accustomed to."

"But they were humans," he inserted, with wry disbelief. "Not demons or mythic half-man, half-beast creatures or alien beings from another planet or dimension?"

"Adam." Her soft voice held a definite note of warning. "If you persist in laughing at me, I…"

"You'll what?" He interrupted in challenge.

"I won't kiss you any more."

Now there was a real serious consideration. Adam controlled the grin twitching on his lips, lips that still retained the taste of her, the feel of her, the sweetness of her eager and hungry mouth.

Laugh and he went kissless.

Adam prudently remained sober.

"That's better." Sunny's eyes sparkled, revealing her amusement. "Shall I go on?"

"Be my guest," he invited—straight-faced.

She glanced pointedly around the cozy sitting room. "I believe I already am."

"Cute."

She laughed. "Now, where was I?"

"With the wild bunch."

"Are you laughing?" she asked in a stern tone, undermined by the gleam in her eyes.

"No," he answered with deceptive solemnity.

"Okay, then. They were *wild* looking," she continued, her lips quivering. "Wild and fierce, pride in their ancient Celtic heritage running hot in their veins. But there were the learned ones, too, and artisans, as well, crafting beautiful jewelry, metalworks and artifacts that are still highly valued and admired today."

"And I suppose I was one of the artisans?" he asked, unable to completely mask his skepticism.

"Oh, no." Sunny shook her head. "You were the strongest, most fearless warrior in our small tribe."

"Tribes, yet," he muttered, concealing the wash of pleasure her assertion afforded him.

"Yes, small groups..." She frowned. "From the little I understood, the tribes consisted of families with a common ancestor. Most of the tribes lived in small rural settlements and raised crops and livestock."

"Not unlike the Native Americans," he mused aloud.

"Yes." Her eyes lit up. "In fact, now that you mention it, there was a similarity."

"You didn't happen to be watching a lot of old western movies on TV prior to your visions?" he asked, suddenly positive he had hit upon the root cause of her supposed past-life memories.

Sunny leveled a withering, pitying look at him. "I said they were similar, not identical, Adam. Besides, the Celtic images were merely the first. Subsequent memories were from other various times and locations.''

''I stand corrected.''

''You're sitting down.''

''Get on with it.'' He made a show of glancing at his wristwatch. ''It's going on nine.''

''But you're the one who interrupted,'' she pointed out with sweet reason.

Adam's uncertain patience ran out. ''Is there by any chance a point to this story—''

Sunny opened her mouth, but Adam wasn't finished.

''And if so, will you get to it?''

''You took me, made me your woman, the summer I turned thirteen.''

''*What?*'' Adam recoiled as if she had physically struck him. ''I never...''

''You did,'' she said, blithely cutting him off. ''But it was not only acceptable—it was expected.''

He scowled.

''Adam, at that period the life expectancy was very short.'' Her brow wrinkled in thought. ''Although I'm not positive, you understand, I think that even those called the elders were probably not much more than fifty, if that.''

While her rationale made sense on the surface, Adam still found the concept troubling. The very idea that he would initiate a mere child was repugnant.

"But...thirteen?" he said, shaking his head in disbelief and negation.

"I was a woman, fully grown and fully developed." Her smile somehow managed to appear both compassionate and sensual. "You were gentle...and wonderful."

"I was?" Adam's voice was rough, and he was unaware of revealing his acceptance of her claim.

"Oh, yes." The tones of compassion were gone, leaving her voice rich with sensuality. "After the first time, the piercing pain and adjustment of your invasion, I loved, craved the feeling of you inside me, the thrilling sensations created by your stroking hands, your mouth suckling at my breasts, your slim, hard body between my thighs."

Oh, sweet agony. Adam's mouth and throat were bone-dry, his palms and forehead damp with sweat. His hardening body was gripped by the delicious ache of arousal. He wanted Sunny, right there, right then, hurt with the need to act out the scenario she had made almost visual with her explicitly descriptive words.

Without thought or pause to reflect, he reached for her, pulling her roughly into his embrace. She came willingly, sighing as he crushed her breasts against his chest.

"I want you, too."

Her murmured confession shattered what was left of his restraint. Adam was too far gone to realize that the vaguely heard growl-like sound came from his own throat. All he knew and understood was the luscious temptation of her mouth, her lips quivering in anticipation, the enticement of the tip of her tongue gliding along the edge of her teeth.

Lowering his head, he fit his mouth to hers, plunged his tongue deep, in a thrust evocative of a fuller, more meaningful possession.

Sunny responded by engaging his tongue in a sensual duel, tasting him as he tasted her.

His heart thumping, Adam thrilled to the possessive curl of her arms around his taut neck, the spear of her slender fingers into his hair.

He had to get closer, closer to her. Tightening his hold on her, Adam slid his aching body over the side of the settee and onto the floor. Sunny made a soft landing on top of him, the juncture of her thighs in contact with his rigid, straining manhood. Her long hair fell forward, curtaining his head in strands of gold-streaked silk.

His mouth clinging to hers, he grasped her by the hips and rolled over, settling his body in the cradle of her thighs. There was the grating sound of ripping, and he knew the skirt seams had given way at the side slits from calf to mid-thigh, for his manhood was suddenly pressed to the mound of her femininity.

It was heaven and it was hell, heaven because it was where he wanted to be, hell because their clothing barred the way to the desired feel of skin on skin.

Adam moved his hands in a restless quest along the sides of her body, skimming the fullness of her breasts, the indentation of her waist, the curve of her hips and bottom. He wanted to touch her everywhere but...

His chest was on fire, his lungs protesting a need to breathe. Reluctantly, he raised his hands to her head, cupping her face as he slid his mouth from hers.

"Yes," she murmured on a heartfelt sigh of relief. "You haven't changed. You are still my hot-blooded, impatient and wonderful lover."

Five

Damn.

Square one.

Adam groaned. This was nuts, he thought, despair dulling the edge of his arousal. This entire experience, from their first encounter in the street to his body pressing hers into the carpet was purely and simply nuts.

But he wanted her more intensely than he had ever before wanted any other woman. The realization was sobering, almost frightening.

Heaving a sigh, Adam rolled off the soft and tempting cushion of Sunny's body and onto his back on the floor beside her. He drew several deep breaths, repeatedly swallowing before attempting to speak.

"I'm going out of my mind here," he muttered, staring at the ceiling. "Totally insane."

"My poor darling," Sunny murmured, pushing herself up into a sitting position. She gazed down at him with eyes softened by compassion. "Acceptance comes hard, I know."

Acceptance wasn't the only thing hard, Adam ridiculed himself in select frustration. Telling himself to get up off the floor, yet lacking the energy to move, he stared at her narrowly, fighting the urge to pull her down on top of him again, lose himself in her cool eyes and hot mouth.

"Adam?"

"Yeah?"

"It's all right." She smiled. "It's natural."

He frowned. "What is?"

"Wanting to be with me, hurting with the need to be joined with me, body and soul."

Geeze. Body *and* soul, yet. The jury's in, he mused. Total insanity, without doubt.

Adam felt torn by conflicting desires, a part of him demanding he play the gentleman, take her home, get her out of his life, while another part of him, a part he didn't recognize, cautioned him against taking a precipitous action that just might impact his entire future.

Rendered inert by the inner conflict, he stared at Sunny in mute appeal.

Her eyes revealing her concern for his personal struggle, Sunny shifted, drawing her legs up closer to her body, exposing her silky thighs through the tear in her skirt seam.

"I'm sorry for causing the rip in your skirt," he muttered. "Of course, I'll pay for the repairs."

"The skirt is unimportant, Adam." She gave the tear a negligent glance. "It's material—" she smiled "—or, in this instance, immaterial."

"What is material, then?"

"You and me and a love centuries old, yet ever new and renewing."

New Age hogwash or... Adam restlessly moved his head, finding comfort in the reality of the carpet fibers scraping against his scalp.

"Sunny, I cannot buy into this concept of reincar—" he began, only to be silenced by the fingers she pressed against his lips.

"It'll take time, love," she said, giving a quick, impatient shake of her head. "I'm moving too fast for you. It took me years to assimilate, believe and accept the memory images."

"A young girl's fairy tales, not memories of past lives," he said, his voice made harsh by disappointment. He jolted up to sit facing her. "Sunny, I doubt I'll ever believe that you and I— or anyone else for that matter—have shared experiences of other lives."

"But you promised."

Oh, hell. Adam detected the onset of a headache, very likely, he presumed, from beating his head against the stone wall of Sunny's persistence.

Feeling his resistance wavering, he ran a thoughtful look over her enticing form. Sunny might be a genuine cuckoo bird, but she certainly was one tempting cuckoo bird.

"Will you allow me to finish my story?" she asked in imploring tones. "All my stories?"

Temptation decided the issue. Raking a hand through his already disheveled hair, Adam surrendered his rational self to his sensual nature.

"Might as well," he said, rising, then offering a hand to help her up. "You've got one week. But for now, I want to hear about this supposed promise."

The smile Sunny blessed him with was almost worth his surrender. Almost, but not quite. Adam didn't, would not grant complete surrender, not even to his damnable sensuous nature, without a fight. On the spot, he decided that Miss Sunny Dase was in for the battle of her life. She would have to struggle mightily for every inch he gave her—literally, as well as figuratively.

As if exhausted by their exchange, Sunny dropped like a stone onto the settee and groped for the glass of wine she had set aside.

Following her lead, Adam settled beside her. Reaching for his own glass, he drained the warm red wine without pausing for breath. The glass empty, he set it down with a thunk, then gave a flick of his hand.

"Please, continue."

A frown crinkled her smooth brow. "Yes... er...where was I, do you recall?"

Adam's smile was blatant with suggestion. "You were loving the feel of my hard body between your thighs." If he had thought to rattle her, and he had, his shot went wide of its intended target.

Sunny's smile was smug with satisfaction. "Yes, and you assumed that position—eagerly and a lot."

The tightness in Adam's body, his loins, had just begun to ease somewhat; her assertion tightened him again like an overwound watch spring.

"Careful, lady," he murmured in warning. "You're stomping on uncertain and shaky ground."

Sunny apparently felt confident enough to laugh at him. Her laughter rippled through the quiet room, swirling around him, an unabrasive, gentle invitation to him to join in, share the moment of mutual enjoyment with her.

Adam couldn't resist her sweet call to amusement. A soft chuckle rumbled in his chest, expanding into a full-throated laugh as it burst from his smiling lips.

"You're a witch," he accused, shaking his head in amused despair at his own weakness.

Sunny mirrored his action, not in despair but in negation of his charge. "No, just a woman," she murmured. "A one-man-forever kind of woman."

Her claim sobered him at once, and laced his voice with cynicism. "You've never been with another man?"

"I didn't say that."

"That's what I thought." Although his voice maintained a cynical edge, Adam felt a perplexing sense of betrayal. He exhaled a harsh breath, unconsciously reflecting the sudden deflated sensation inside his body and mind. Knowing it was irrational, if not plain stupid, he felt hurt, wounded by her admission, and he wanted to lash out, inflict pain on her in retaliation. "Doesn't say much for the loyalty of a forever kind of woman, does it?"

"Oh, Adam," Sunny murmured, her smile gently chiding. "Still quick to jealously and judgment?"

"What do you mean?" he snapped, uncomfortably recalling the flashes of jealously he'd felt over her innocent exchange with the waiter at dinner.

Her smile taunted. "Your ongoing tendency toward possessiveness."

A denial sprang to Adam's lips. Self-knowledge kept him from uttering it. Her assertion was true, as far as it went. He was possessive, and protective, about his family and their jointly owned corporation. But Adam had never in his life experienced even a twinge of jealousy, never mind a streak of possessiveness in regard to a woman. And the only woman he had ever felt protective of was his mother.

"I have never been jealous, judgmental or possessive of any woman," he said with cool conviction.

"Maybe not," she responded with unruffled calm. "At least, not this time around."

Around. And around. And around, Adam thought, beginning to feel a mite dizzy. Time to get off this particular merry-go-round.

"Finish your story," he said, suppressing a sigh of weariness—or was it regret?

"We had two wonderful years together." Once again, Sunny startled him with the abruptness of her launch into her recitation. "Two years of loving and laughter in relative peace and prosperity."

"And then?" Adam prompted, made anxious by the sorrow that dimmed, darkened her eyes.

"We, our tribe, were under attack."

Though she continued to look straight at him, Adam had the distinct and uneasy sensation that Sunny no longer saw him but a scene visible only to her.

"The smoke and scent of our cooking fires drew a Roman patrol to our campsite." She blinked, and focused on him. A smile of sad acceptance curved her soft lips. "You rallied our warriors. Fighting fiercely, you drove them off...then followed in hot pursuit."

Something in her tone, her expression, instilled a sense of dread in Adam. "Go on," he said, spurred on by a ballooning urgency.

"You didn't come back."

The pervasive dread inside Adam stilled his thoughts, dried his throat. "Wh-why not?" he asked in a raw whisper, hating the unsteadiness of his voice, yet unable to control the fearful tremor.

Sunny's eyes were wide, staring; staring at scenes only she could visualize.

"Why not?" Adam's voice was stronger, harsh with a demand for an answer.

"Many of our warriors were slain," she said in tones of sheer agony. "The few that managed to escape stumbled, wounded and bleeding, into camp. They reported that you had been captured by the invaders."

"Go on," Adam urged, shaken by the expression of horror in her staring eyes.

"Our remaining tribe members were shocked and enraged, unable to believe our bravest had been torn from us."

Her eyes glittered with a strange light, a look of madness that caused a clenching sensation in Adam. He opened his mouth to ask her to continue, but no words came.

"I was distraught, crazed," she went on, her voice growing stronger with emotional fury. "I snatched a sword from the wounded bloody hand of a warrior, and ran screaming from the campsite, vowing vengeance."

Good Lord. Without conscious thought, Adam

pressed back against the settee, distancing himself from the hate blazing from Sunny's eyes.

"They stopped me," she said, her voice a gritty, snarling cry of resentment. "The elders, the women, my aged parents, caught me and brought me back." Her eyes were wild, terrifying. "Oh, I fought them. Kicking and screaming invectives, calling upon our gods to intercede, I fought them. But there were too many, and they subdued me. At first I had to be physically restrained, to keep me from running again, to find your abductors, to kill and be killed."

"Sunny," he said sharply, repelled by the pure malice firing her eyes.

She lowered her head. A shudder rippled the length of her slender body. When she raised her head moments later, her eyes were clear of the blistering hate but dark, dark green pools of unspeakable sorrow.

"And..." Adam had to pause to swallow, moisten his parched throat. "And then?"

"All the fight went out of me and I withdrew inside myself." Sunny sighed; it made a heart-wrenching sound. "I lay for some months, listless and uncaring. I was unaware and unconcerned when the decision was made to strike camp, move on to a hopefully safer location closer to the sea."

Adam frowned. "The sea?"

"Yes...somewhere along the Brittany coast." Sunny's voice was dull, as unconcerned as she claimed to have been. "My mother and the women of the tribe cared for me, or I surely would have starved to death, as I had longed to do."

"*No.*" The protest erupted from his throat.

"Yes." Her smile pained him. "It was the first faint movements of the babe that cleared my mind, brought me back to my senses."

Adam jolted. "Babe?"

"Yes. I was with child..." Sunny stared directly into his startled eyes. "Your child."

A child. *His* child. Suddenly, Adam felt as though he couldn't breathe, as if his chest was being compressed, squeezing all the air from his body. The mere act of speaking, forming the words seemed an insurmountable task. Yet for some inexplicable reason, his mind demanded he ask, know the sex of the child she claimed was his.

"A...a...son or a...daughter?" he finally managed to squeak through his constricted throat.

Sunny's eyes. Her eyes. Those beautiful, expressive, mountain-glen-green eyes had the power to claw at his heart and soul with the depths of their reflected sadness.

"I don't know...and therein lies the tragedy."

"Explain," he cried, so enmeshed in her tale, he was numb to the fact of being caught up in it. "What tragedy?"

She exhaled another shattering sigh. "There was a man, another warrior of our tribe, your friend and soul brother. He had survived the fray, although he had been sorely wounded. He approached my parents, offered to take me to wife, raise your child as his own.''

Once again that flame of jealousy flared hot and bright inside Adam, shocking him with its intensity. Making a concentrated effort, he tamped it down enough to ask with a degree of steadiness, ''You accepted?''

''No!'' Sunny exclaimed, giving a violent shake of her head. ''I was your woman...yours alone.''

While Adam felt somewhat shamed by the sense of relief that washed over him, he felt an equal sense of satisfaction on hearing her declare herself as *his* woman. Pitiable as he knew himself to be, he savored the thrill just the same.

''But the tragedy you mentioned...?''

''My parents gratefully accepted your friend's offer.'' A tired smile shadowed her lips. ''They hastened to arrange for the ceremony, because by then my body was big with your growing child.'' Her eyes grew stormy, reflecting the rebellion fermenting her thoughts. ''I could not bear it, could not tolerate the thought of a man, however kind and good, other than you, laying between my thighs.''

''But what could you do?'' Adam asked, denying himself another thrill at her assertion. ''What could you possibly do to prevent the ceremony and the subsequent results?''

Sunny's eyes narrowed, sending a premonitory

shiver through him. When at last she spoke, her voice was low, her tone dangerous, her words measured. "I pleaded with my parents to reverse their decision, and when they refused in the cause of doing what was best for me I flung myself from the cliffs, into the waves crashing onto the shore below."

"Good God." Stunned, Adam's voice was little more than a shocked whisper.

She didn't seem to hear. "I lived for two days after they discovered me on the beach, my broken body in agony, injured muscles straining in desperate contraction to expel the babe from my womb."

His throat constricted, unable to speak, Adam reached out to grasp her hands; they felt like ice.

Tears welled in her eyes and flowed down her cheeks. "Vitally alive and glowing with an inner light, you knelt beside my—our—sleeping pallet mere hours before I died."

"What?" Adam unknowingly crushed her hands with his tight grip. Her wince brought him to the realization that he was hurting her and he eased his grip. "What?" he repeated, shaking his head. "Had I escaped my captors?"

"No." Sunny shook her head, seeming to accept as natural his apparent suspension of skepticism. "During the long months of your captivity, you had come to accept their Christian beliefs and their Savior. In a show of trust, they allowed you to leave, accepting your vow to return with your wife.''

"But you...you were..." Adam halted, every cell inside him cringing against giving voice to the fact, real or imagined, of her death.

"Yes, I was dying," she said with utter calm. "And I somehow knew the babe was already dead." Her somber gaze caressed his tension-taut features. "You wept—your tears mingled with mine on my cheeks. And then, moments before my death, you made a solemn vow to me, in the name of your newly embraced deity, whom you proclaimed was the One True God." Her fantastic eyes held his startled gaze.

"My promise," he whispered, unmindful of the tremor in his voice, and in his fingers curled around hers.

"Yes, your promise."

"For God's sake, Sunny, tell me," he said in a harsh croak. "What was it?"

"Invoking His name, you promised, swore to me that we would be together again and throughout eternity."

Six

It was very late. The stillness of darkness held the night in thrall. Inside the dimly lit motel room, nervous tension kept Adam active, moving.

It was nuts.

The thought had resounded in his head ever since he had returned hours earlier to pace the room after driving an obviously exhausted Sunny to the apartment she shared with another female reenactor, located above a camera shop scant blocks from the restored area.

The certainty of the craziness of Sunny's tale of a bygone life, or lives as she'd have him believe, wiped away any hope he had harbored for a solid night's slumber.

It had to be craziness or else…

Adam raked his long fingers through his hair, ruffling the already disheveled strands.

If it wasn't craziness, then… He grimaced against the doubting thought and the sour taste at the back of his throat. The concept was too far-out to bear thinking about.

But Sunny…with her hot mouth and her eager body and her near declaration of undying love—for him.

Now, there was a concept not easily dismissed.

Adam's lips twisted in wry self-knowledge. He had felt an instantaneous attraction to her, which in itself was not all that unusual; he had felt an instant attraction to members of the opposite sex before.

But never before had the attraction escalated so rapidly into a desire so strong, so intense it bordered on near desperation.

He had to have her, possess her, be one with her. The extent of the need, the hunger he felt for her came damn close to frightening Adam; it was too akin to what he had heard about the cravings of addicts for a narcotic fix.

What was it with Sunny, anyway? He asked himself, absently traversing the distance between the sitting-room window and the connecting bedroom. What was it about her, in particular, that struck a chord inside him?

If he were of a fanciful nature, which Adam

most decidedly was not, he might conclude their mutual attraction had been fated or preordained. Sunny had made her beliefs on that score crystal clear.

But undying love, a shared love throughout eternity?

Ridiculous.

Shaking his head, Adam retraced his path to the sitting-room window.

Reincarnation.

Yeah. Right. An ongoing love for all time, all seasons, he mocked in silent disbelief. How had Sunny expressed it? All their seasons past.

New Age gobbledygook, Adam told himself. If he had any sense, he'd run, not walk away from any further involvement with the flight-of-fancy-prone Ms. Sunny Dase.

That being the case, he ruminated, why had he sought and received her agreement to have dinner with him again tomorrow evening? No, *this* evening, Adam corrected himself, groaning as he glanced at his wristwatch.

The answer to that one was easy. He didn't want to run or walk away from further involvement with Sunny—strange as she might be. On the contrary, what he wanted, felt compelled to do, was deepen his involvement with her.

Adam gave a derisive snort: in all truth, what he really wanted was to take her to bed.

And Sunny was willing, exceedingly willing.

So why shouldn't he? Surely he could overlook her oddness, listen unjudgmentally to her promised retelling of their supposed next incarnation together, to reap the reward of being with her, in the position she herself claimed they had enjoyed a lot?

Desire rekindled, sizzling through Adam. Conversely, at the same time, weariness dragged at his eyelids and his mind.

Oh, what the hell, he mused, not bothering to stifle a wide yawn. Sunny was exciting, if slightly strange, more exciting than any woman he had met to date. He'd go with the flow, he decided, see what developed. If nothing else, she was entertaining, and he was looking forward to seeing her again, their evening together.

Get some sleep, Romeo, he advised himself, trudging into the bedroom and flinging himself fully dressed onto the bed. Knowing he wouldn't be up to anything later, physically or mentally, if he didn't get some rest, he shut his eyes, certain slumber would elude him.

Adam was dead to the world within minutes.

The eyes were piercing.

A captive of the portrait executed so compellingly by the artist, Adam stared into the lifelike direct gaze of the dark eyes of Patrick Henry. Of all the paintings adorning the walls of the large room inside the capitol building in the restored area, Adam had been inexorably drawn to the riveting eyes of the patriot's likeness.

The soft, drawling voice of the reenactor recounting the historical events that had taken place in the original capitol prior to the Revolutionary War penetrated Adam's consciousness, drawing him from his mesmerized state.

The portrait was incredible. Adam had the sensation he could almost hear the orator's impassioned voice arguing, imploring, demanding freedom or death.

Of course, Adam knew Henry's famous cry had rung out in Richmond, not in Williamsburg or even Philadelphia, as many believed. Nevertheless, the firebrand's words resounded inside Adam's mind and heart as he trailed the group he had joined for the guided tour through the capitol building.

Outside, another large group milled around the entrance, eagerly awaiting admittance into the building.

"Good afternoon, ladies and gentlemen. Welcome to the capitol. If you would be so kind as to follow me...?"

A smile tugged at Adam's lips as he strolled away; these reenactors were exceptionally good. The restoration of Colonial Williamsburg had to have been a phenomenal project. But the results certainly proved worth the effort. Everything appeared real and current. One could not help but feel as though one had literally stepped back in time.

A feeling of well-being settled inside Adam as he sauntered down Duke of Gloucester Street. Though his pace was leisurely, his eyes were busy admiring the simple beauty of the Christmas decorations, all constructed from nature's bounty of greens and fruits and nuts, adorning most of the buildings.

While admiring the decorations, the thought occurred to Adam that although the Christmas season had very definite appeal, he couldn't help feeling Independence Day might be even more meaningful to him, resonate with his deeply felt, if seldom voiced patriotism, pride in his beloved country.

But by whim or twist of fate, since he happened to be there at the moment, he intended to enjoy the visit. Perhaps he'd come back again sometime, at another season, to celebrate the Fourth of July holiday.

Although the day was overcast, and some ten degrees cooler than the previous afternoon, the sidewalks were crowded, the shops and other buildings open to the public enjoying a steady stream of sightseers.

It was Adam's first full day in the restored area, and he intended to make the most of it, even though he had had a late start.

He had overslept, not surprisingly since he hadn't dropped off to sleep until near dawn. But the dreamless slumber had refreshed him and he had awakened with an unaccustomed eagerness to explore what was in effect every American's heritage, one of the fountainheads of the concept of independence and liberty.

After a quick shower, Adam made do with a sparse breakfast of juice, coffee and toast. He was looking forward to having lunch in one of the inns in the restored area, and didn't want to blunt his appetite.

Strolling along, he followed a small group of tourists into the tiny apothecary shop. Minutes later, Adam retreated, shuddering in response to the listing of archaic curatives on the shelves, being explained by the bespectacled reenactor stationed behind the counter.

Two houses down from the apothecary, he followed another larger group for a guided tour of the Raleigh Tavern, marveling along with everyone else at the cramped quarters the overnight guests—amongst whom were included George Washington and Thomas Jefferson—had endured.

Envisioning the roomy suite he'd engaged at the motel, and comparing it to the crude conditions of the large sleeping rooms at the tavern, which had housed not one but numerous guests on any given night, Adam reflected that though the historical period had its charm, he'd take the amenities of twentieth-century America hands down.

Adam was tempted to follow the group, and the

delicious aromas tickling his nose, into the Raleigh Tavern bakeshop, but prudence and the consideration of unnecessary calories prevailed.

Forging ahead, he went on to the silversmith's shop. There, Adam succumbed to temptation, selecting beautifully handcrafted Christmas gifts—tie bars for his brothers, delicate earrings for his sister.

The next shop housed the milliner. Deciding to give the headgear a pass, Adam stopped at the corner intersecting Duke of Gloucester with Botetourt Street, to consult his map of the restored area.

According to the map, he was walking south on the north side of Duke of Gloucester. Located in the next block was the shop of one M. Dubois, grocer, the printing office and the colonial post office. In the block after that was the Prentis Store. And in the following block was the larger edifice of Chowning's Tavern.

Adam's stomach growled. One of his acquaintances had sung the praises of the cold potato-leek soup and hearty sandwiches served at Chowning's.

Hungry, yet interested in seeing the printing office and the post office, Adam hesitated. A chill drop of rain striking his cheek decided the issue; he strode across the street, heading directly for the tavern.

The potato-leek soup and baked Virginia ham and Swiss cheese sandwich exceeded Adam's expectations. The full-bodied burgundy he sipped between bites enhanced the flavors. While savoring every morsel and sip, Adam studied his map.

There was so much to see spread out over the area. Opting to be systematic, he decided to take in the sights available on the north side of Duke of Gloucester Street, which included Bruton Parish Church and the Governor's Palace—Adam was particularly looking forward to the palace.

His appetite appeased, Adam exited the tavern and came to a dead stop on the covered porch. It was raining, not just a gentle drizzle but a steady downpour. And the air temperature appeared to have dropped at least ten degrees.

Observing the tourists scurrying along the street and sidewalks, he pondered his options. Rain didn't bother him. On the other hand, his excellent lunch had left him feeling mellow and lethargic.

He glanced at his watch, surprised to note he had lingered over an hour at lunch. It was two-fifteen. He was to pick up Sunny at five forty-five in order to get to the King's Arms Tavern for their six o'clock reservation.

And the rain continued to pelt the tourists rushing along in search of shelter.

A dollar against a plug nickel the rain was cold, Adam thought, observing the hunched shoulders and turned-up collars on most of the people hurrying past.

The idea of standing, wet and cold and shivering, inside any of the exhibits decided the issue for Adam.

Shrugging, he reasoned an afternoon nap would better prepare him for whatever Sunny had in store for him after dinner. Consulting the map once again, he figured his route back to the hotel. By walking one block south on Queen to Francis Street, then heading east, he'd connect with York Street, leading to Route 60 and the motel.

Folding the map, he flipped up the collar on his jacket, hunched his shoulders and dashed into the rain, joining the steady flow of pedestrian traffic.

Adam was loping along, his long strides eating up the sidewalk on Francis Street, when a sign on a shop front caught his notice, stopping him in his tracks.

Gunsmith?

Adam frowned. "Wrong," he murmured, unaware he spoke aloud. "That's not where it was then."

A shiver unrelated to the cold rain trickled down his spine. How had he known the shop was in the wrong location? He still hadn't read any of the written material provided at the visitors' center. And he had been concentrating his study of the map on the exhibits located on the north side of Duke of Gloucester Street; the gunsmith's shop, at least *this* gunsmith shop, was situated to the south of Duke of Gloucester.

Yet, not one doubt assailed Adam; he *knew* the

location was incorrect...for whatever reason of the layout planners.

Standing stock-still in the pouring rain, the surface chill as nothing compared to the cold sensation inside, Adam stared at the building, while his inner eye saw another shop, the original shop, located north of Duke of Gloucester.

How? How could he know, be so certain? Adam asked himself, tearing his riveted gaze away and continuing on along the street, if at a much slower pace. How, unless...

Unless he had been there before.

The unthinkable thought spurred him into action; Adam took off like a sprinter, running all the way back to the motel. He came to an abrupt halt at the entranceway, drew several deep breaths, then, controlling the urge to hurry, he strolled through the lobby to the elevators.

He was visibly shivering by the time he shut the door to the suite behind him.

Telling himself he was shivering because he was soaked and cold, and of a certainty not because of the misplaced location of the damned gun shop, Adam began stripping off his wet garments as he made for the bedroom and the connecting bath.

With his clothes tossed in a soggy heap on the floor, he stepped into the steamy shower. While the hot water pounded the top of his head, quick, questioning thoughts beat against the inside of his aching skull.

How had he known about the gun shop?

Come to that, why was he positive he was right?

Was he right?

But if he was right, could Sunny's claim be true?

Were such concepts as reincarnation and love everlasting possible?

Or was he going loony tunes, losing touch with reality?

Seven

It was still raining, harder than before. The in-
clement weather hadn't kept the diners from the
tavern.

The King's Arms had an air of elegance, an am-
bience of the gentility of an earlier age.

Adam barely noticed. Distracted, not only by
the incident of the gunsmith's shop that afternoon
but also by the effect of Sunny's appearance on
his senses, he noted the refined eighteenth-century
decor, heard the polite, almost flowery speech of
the costumed waiters and waitresses—serving
maids?—and yet registered very little of it.

Sunny, attired in a flowing soft wool plaid skirt,
starched white cotton shirt and tartan vest, had sto-

len Adam's breath and scrambled his gray matter from the moment she answered his knock on her apartment door.

Seated opposite her at a small table set in a corner of what he presumed to be the main dining room of the tavern, he was blind to his surroundings, his attention riveted on the picture of enticing femininity she presented to the world in general and Adam in particular.

The contrast was so very startling from the way she had looked when he had driven her home the previous night. Then, she had looked shattered, as if emotionally ravaged by the reliving or at least the retelling of her supposed memories. Her glorious eyes had been dull, lifeless, the delicate soft skin beneath appearing bruised, her face pale and drawn.

Now, Sunny's appearance reflected her name. Her cheeks glowed with the becoming flush of vibrant life, her eyes sparkled with animation.

Unlike the night before, she had not let her glorious gold-streaked brown mane flow unbound and free. She had pulled it away from her face, not into a careless topknot but smoothed back and folded into a classic French twist.

Adam's fingers literally itched to pluck the pins from the twist, freeing the mass to allow his fingers free reign to stroke and comb through the silken strands.

A sizzling arrow of desire seared him. Clenching his muscles in reaction to the inner flame, he drew a deep breath and told himself to get a grip.

Granted, Sunny was a beautiful woman but... Adam's gaze tangled in the forest-glade depths of her eyes; his breath lodged in his aching throat.

There was no doubt about it: she was utterly captivating, so much so that Adam forgot the odd sense of déjà vu he had experienced that afternoon, and that he had planned to question her about the location, current and previous, of the gunsmith's shop. He forgot her reputed flights of fancy. He forgot the odd feelings he'd had while she had been spinning her tale the night before. He forgot everything.

"The soup."

"I beg your pardon?" Adam blinked himself from his reverie; although his gaze had been centered upon the movement of her soft, luscious mouth, he had not comprehended a word she had uttered.

Sunny smiled, that maddening, all-knowing smile. "I said, you should try the specialties of the house, most particularly the soup."

"Soup?" Frowning, he made a dedicated effort to pull his scattered thoughts together.

She nodded. "The peanut soup." She grinned at the skeptical look he gave her. "Really, it's delicious."

"Uh-huh," he murmured, perusing the menu. "Do you have any other recommendations?"

"The game pie," she said at once. "And, oh yes, you can't pass up the Sally Lunn."

"Who or what is a Sally Lunn?"

Sunny's laugh was soft and completely enchanting. "Sally Lunn is a bread."

"Oh."

"There's also a drink specialty," she went on, laughter dancing at the edges of her voice. "A wine, somewhat like sangria, flavored with fruit and…"

"I'll pass," Adam interjected, lifting his shoulders in a half shrug. "I prefer a burgundy," he said, mentally asking himself, *since when?*

"Of course." Her voice was serene with acceptance. "While I, as you know, prefer a white wine."

The damn thing was, Adam *did* know, and it was a knowing much deeper and more intricately involved than her choice of white wine the night before.

Sunny never drank any form of spirits other than a light, dry white wine.

Dammit. How had he known that?

The certainty of the knowledge was disconcerting at best and unnerving at worst.

"Adam?"

"Hmm?" he murmured, collecting his wits—or whatever was left of them. "What?"

"Don't."

He frowned. "Don't what?"

She smiled. "Don't torment yourself. Later, after dinner, we'll discuss it."

Adam didn't require an explanation of what *it* she referred to: he knew full well, too well.

He heaved a sigh and tried to avoid the issue by bringing up another one. "I distinctly recall you saying you would treat me to the second one of your stories this evening."

"And I will." Her eyes, those intelligent, so expressive green eyes gleamed with teasing intent. "But that was a rather dull, unexciting go-round, so I'll be brief." A tremor of amusement shivered on her tone. "Then we'll discuss this dilemma you're experiencing."

The peanut soup, the game pie and the Sally Lunn all lived up to Sunny's recommendations; the burgundy was excellent, rich and full-bodied.

Surprisingly, Adam enjoyed the meal, despite his feelings of trepidation in regard to Sunny's stated intention to discuss his dilemma.

The only dilemma he wanted to discuss happened to be of a more earthy, sensual nature. He longed to tell her to forget all the silliness about memories and images, previous lives lived and a love for eternity.

Adam considered himself a realist; his interest was focused on the here and the now. And for him, the here and the now was centered on the need, quickly expanding into near obsession, to lose himself within her.

The taste he had had of Sunny the night before had merely whetted his appetite. By the time they had finished dinner and returned to his suite in the motel, Adam was past ready for the entrée of pure Sunshine.

"What was it that bothered you about the gunsmith shop?" she asked, mirroring her actions of the night before by draping her cape over a chair on her way to the window.

Damn, Adam grumbled to himself; he had convinced himself he had succeeded in concealing his involuntary shiver at the sight of the shop as they drove past.

Sunny turned to give him a quizzical look, when he didn't immediately respond.

"Adam?"

Oh, hell, he thought, raking a hand through his rain-dampened hair. Now what? There was no way in hell he could admit to Sunny—of all people—that he had experienced a déjà vu moment. So, then, how to respond?

The rain.

The old inspiration born of desperation, Adam reflected, offering her a benign smile.

"I didn't want to say anything, but in my desire to protect you from the rain in our dash from the inn to the parking lot, I gave the lion's share of the umbrella to you," he explained in gentle, if slightly smug terms. "The shiver you noticed was in reaction to a trickle of cold rain that found its way under my collar and down my spine."

Adam felt rather proud of his hastily concocted excuse; but his moment of pride was short-lived.

"Oh. I see." Sunny's tone was bland, unrevealing. Not so her smile. As it had the night before, her smile gave clear indication she certainly did see, right through him and his fabricated tale.

"Ahh...yeah," he said, frowning in counterpoint to her all-knowing smile. "Would you like a drink?"

"Not right now," she replied, her smile taking on a mocking cast. "Would you like to change your shirt?"

Damn, he thought.

"No," he answered, asking himself if this smiling, silently mocking woman could possibly be the same woman he had supported to his car the previous night, the very same woman who had seemed so very fragile and vulnerable.

Yeah, fragile and vulnerable, he ridiculed, scanning her glowingly beautiful face, her bright expressive eyes, her elegantly erect posture. She appeared, this night, about as fragile and vulnerable as the fearless warrior she had claimed him to be in her story.

"You're looking stormier than the weather," Sunny observed, raising delicately arched eyebrows over her watchful green eyes. "What are you thinking?"

"That it's time to get down to business," he prevaricated, indicating the settee with a flick of a hand. "I'm waiting with bated breath for your second past-life story."

"Sure you are," she drawled, laughing openly at him. "I submit that you are about as eager to hear my story as you would be to have a root canal."

Nevertheless, to his grateful relief, she didn't pursue his motives. Slipping out of her shoes, she strolled to the settee and curled up in one corner, in precisely the same position as the night before.

Adam did not follow suit. Instead, he strolled to the drinks cabinet and broke the seal. "Sure you don't want a drink?" he asked, in precisely the same manner as he had before. "To keep your throat moist during the relating of your... memories?"

"No, thank you." She gave a quick shake of her head, drawing his glance to the light shimmering in the gold strands of her hair. "As I mentioned, I won't require much time or emotional effort in the telling."

"Your choice." Adam shrugged. "But if you don't mind, I think I'll have one...just in case I suddenly find myself in need of fortification."

"I don't mind at all," she assured him, smiling as she settled more comfortably into the settee.

Without conscious direction, he reached into the cabinet and withdrew a small bottle of cabernet— the only red wine available—and poured it into one of the stemmed glasses set atop the cabinet. He took a sip of the ruby wine before ambling to the settee…and damned if he wasn't really beginning to appreciate the flavor.

"Whenever you're ready," he invited her to begin as he seated himself opposite her.

"It's really a rather dull story," she said, as if compelled to give warning.

"You mean, there was no reveling, a lot, in a certain intimate position?" Adam asked, wincing inside at the offensiveness of his drawling voice, the content of his query.

To his surprise, Sunny didn't take offense. Quite the contrary. Her sudden burst of easy laughter gave evidence of genuine amusement.

"No, that isn't what I mean," she said when her laughter subsided. "The existence itself was dull and uninteresting, not the intimate part of it."

Adam heaved a sigh of defeat. "I suppose I had better hear the entire story."

"Right," she agreed, her eyes dancing, her lips twitching. "Well, once upon a time, long, long ago…oh, two or so hundred years after our first life together…"

Adam halted her narrative by groaning aloud.

Sunny arched one elegant eyebrow. "I thought you wanted to hear this story?"

"I do, I do," he muttered, taking a bracing swallow of his wine. "Flourishes and all."

"Then please refrain from interrupting," she chided, scowling, in conflict to her laughing eyes. "Now, I don't know if you're at all familiar with that historical period, but it was pretty grim...not a fun time for peasants."

"We were peasants?" Adam sounded offended, simply because he felt offended. He headed up a fairly sizable family corporation. Considering his position and extremely generous income, if he had to be labeled, it would have to be upper, upper middle class. Peasants indeed.

"Primarily, there were the rulers and the serfs, Adam," she pointed out, her taunting voice snaring his wandering attention. "Other than the in-between merchants, there weren't a whole lot of upper, middle or lower-middle income groups littering the landscape."

"Hmm," he murmured, lacking the brass to admit he preferred to fancy himself as one of the rulers. "And where did this charming existence take place?"

"Britain." Though her voice held conviction, Sunny frowned. "I don't know exactly where in Britain, but I feel certain it was Britain."

He looked skeptical.

She shrugged and continued. "We mated young...life expectancy was still very short," she added, anticipating his objection.

He objected anyway, strongly. "You again have me cast in the role of defiler of young girls?"

"Honestly, Adam." Sunny rolled her eyes. "It was not only accepted, it was necessary. A couple started young...in hopes of seeing their offspring grow to maturity."

"Point taken," he conceded, reluctantly.

"We were farmers..."

"Wonderful."

"Adam!"

He held up his hand. "I'll shut up."

"Good." She gave a long-suffering sigh. "We lived in a small cottage...actually little more than a hut, located outside a tiny village. Tilling the fields was rudimentary, the farm implements crude. The work was backbreakingly hard. The days were endlessly long. Life was pitifully short."

"Okay, I've got the picture," he said, with more truth than he was willing to admit, for in truth, his imagination conjured the scene and it wasn't pretty. "Go on."

"We died."

"Huh?" Adam jolted, slopping the wine over the edge of the glass and onto his expensive pants. He barely noticed. "You mean, that's all?"

Sunny took a moment to frown at the red stain spreading into the material covering his taut thigh. "You really should remove those pants and soak them in cold water before the stain sets,'' she advised.

He ignored her and the stain. "That's all?'' he repeated, his tone incredulous.

"Well, although we lost several—'' she frowned "—I think it was three babies…''

"We lost them?'' he dared to interrupt again, shocked by the very idea of *losing* a child. "How?''

"Well, not in the woods,'' she retorted in obvious exasperation. "We lost them in the way common to the period, of course, to childhood diseases.''

"Oh…well…in that case…'' He shrugged.

"But we did produce four children who lived to adulthood,'' she said in consoling tones. "Three handsome, tall and stalwart sons and one beautiful daughter.''

"Then we did assume the intimate position quite a lot,'' he murmured, his voice a little rough, husky.

"Oh, yes.'' The brightness in Sunny's eyes darkened, as if shadowed by sensuous memories. "Other than the joy of watching the fruit of your seed grow strong and healthy, my happiest moments occurred when your hard body lay between my thighs, your shaft buried to the hilt inside me.''

A flash fire of desire roared through Adam, and he was forced to apply every ounce of control he possessed to remain still, keep from closing the small space between them to throw his swiftly hardening body atop hers, reenact the erotic scene she had described.

"The physical loving and the laughing we shared, as a couple, then a family, kept the existence from seeming one of unremitting toil." Her soft voice again corralled his thoughts—his inflamed thoughts. She sighed, and a small, pleasurable smile curved her lips. "Though the day-by-day living of it was dull," she went on in a quiet, faraway sounding tone. "The loving was ever exciting and wonderful."

Adam could barely breathe for the tightness in his chest, the thudding of his heart. The die was cast, and Sunny herself had cast it. He had to have her, experience for himself the joy of loving she so vividly recounted.

Moving slowly, so as not to startle her from her reverie, he set his glass aside, then briefly paused, surprised to note the tremor in his fingers.

"Sunny." His voice was slightly unsteady, low, little more than a whisper.

"Hmm?" She raised slumberous eyes to his.

"Come to me." He held out his arms in invitation. "Please. Come love with me."

Without question or hesitation, Sunny slid over the settee to him, into his embrace like a pigeon at long last coming home to roost.

Eight

Their first kiss was gentle, sweet and not nearly enough to satisfy.

Still, not wanting to introduce a jarring note, Adam tested and tasted Sunny's mouth with tentative care, tamping down the urge to crush her lips with his own, plunge his tongue into the honeyed depths of her mouth.

He was on fire, burning with an unprecedented need to be one with her, quench the blaze inside her.

His grasp on control slipped, and even as he silently condemned himself, Adam fastened his mouth to hers, deepening the kiss, filling himself with the delicate wine-scented breath of her life, her unique essence.

Sunny's response was immediate and electrifying. With a soft moan, she speared her fingers into his hair to draw him closer and eagerly parted her lips to receive the piercing stab of his tongue.

Heat, bright and glittery, shimmered inside Adam. He moved his hands, needing to touch her, know her.

But he did know her.

The errant thought shot a lucid strand into the unraveling skein of his mental process.

But the thought was not errant, it was true. His hands recognized the familiar terrain of her slender body, her enticing curves, the fullness of her breasts, the narrowness of her waist, the tight roundness of her derriere and the long, smooth suppleness of her legs.

The realization dropped a cooling cloud of caution over Adam's inflamed senses.

Though he had met this woman just yesterday, he knew her, better, more intimately than he had ever known or cared to know any other woman he had ever been with.

The knowing gave Adam pause to reflect.

She was everything, no, more than he had ever yearned for in the most secret corners of his mind and heart.

She was the soul mate he had been waiting for…and had never dared hope he would find.

Another realization washed over Adam on a

cresting wave of self-knowledge and understanding.

He had been waiting for Sunny.

With his mouth barely touching hers, feeling her warm breath caressing his lips, hearing the soft sounds of pleasure from deep in her throat, Adam felt elated by her precious presence and shaken by the self-realization.

Without conscious awareness he now knew that, since reaching adulthood, with every woman he had known, intimately and socially, he had been waiting for, searching for, longing for Sunny, the other half of himself.

And Sunny was subject to flights of fancy.

It was enough to make a grown man weep, and more than enough to completely bank the fire of desire raging inside him.

Adam could no more suppress a sigh, then stop breathing. He didn't even try.

"Adam?"

Her voice was muffled by his mouth; he heard her just the same, and knew that he would always hear her.

Releasing her mouth, he drew his head back, to stare down, down, down into the emotion-swirled green depths of her incredible, heart-rendingly beautiful eyes.

"Yes?" he responded, beyond believing he would ever find the strength to say no to her, for any reason.

"Will you tell me—now—what bothered you about the gunsmith's shop?"

On second thought, perhaps he would say no to her.

Adam settled for a halfway measure.

"It was nothing, unimportant," he lied in desperation, lowering his head to seek again the singular sweetness of her parted lips and to divert both her persistent question and his unsettling thoughts.

Sunny turned her head to avoid his mouth. Her lips brushed his ear. "It was something," she murmured, sending a shiver of delight and expectation skipping through him from his ear to the suddenly tingling soles of his feet. "And it was important...to you, to me...to us."

Another deeper shiver went skipping along his nervous system in response to her feathering breath and her whispered declaration.

Us. Adam liked the sound of it, the intimacy of it, the permanence of it.

Now, if only he could convince her to wake up to reality, abandon her dreams and imaginings of other lives shared, other loves consummated, otherworldly New Age beliefs of an eternity of togetherness.

The here and now was all he asked or hoped for. Why wasn't that enough for her?

Employing a strength he didn't know he owned, he gently grasped her shoulders and set her back, away from him. He immediately felt cold and lonely.

"Adam?" Sunny's eyes mirrored the chill loneliness he was experiencing.

"I think we'd better slow down. Things are getting too hot too fast." Had he actually said that? Adam could barely believe the cool sound of his own voice, never mind the blatant untruth of his words. Slow down? When he felt his very life might depend on being one with her?

Had he slipped a mental cog or what?

"Slow down?" Confusion clouded Sunny's eyes, dimming their green luster. "But I thought that you wanted..." She hesitated, moistened her lips, then continued in an uncertain whisper... "What I want."

"I do." He grasped her hands, laced his fingers through hers, thrilling to the friction of her soft skin against his toughened, rougher skin. "But...I don't want to rush into anything," he said, while his mind jeered, *liar.*

"But..." Sunny began in protest, but determined to have his say, Adam didn't let her finish.

"We only met yesterday." Impossible. Adam shook his head; had it really only been one day? "We have the rest of the week to explore this physical attraction between us." Oh, brother. He sounded like a stuffy, inexperienced jerk, he upbraided himself. Nevertheless, he stumbled on. "Let's get to know each other first."

"But we do know each other," Sunny protested in agitated exasperation. "We know all the basics about each other. Whereas you have blocked the memories from your consciousness, I remember our being together."

"Fantasy," he snapped, releasing her hands.

"Adam....no...you don't believe..."

Feeling pressured, stressed, not only by her insistence but by his own niggling doubts, Adam silenced her by leaping up to pace the room, raking a hand through his hair. "Yes," he said, giving her a hard stare. "I believe that what you believe to be memories of previous lives lived are merely the love fantasies created inside a young girl's fertile imagination." He drew a quick breath, but went on when she tried to interrupt. "I'm flattered by your having cast me into the role of your heroic fantasy lover, but..."

"You're sounding like a jerk," she finally managed to cut in, decidedly unflatteringly.

Having his own self-assessment endorsed didn't exactly thrill Adam. In fact, he felt insulted, and deep down more than a little hurt.

In a manner he recognized as typically male, he straightened to his full over-six-foot height and leveled a cool, remote and deliberately superior look at her.

"Well, in that case, I'll be happy to take you home," he said, condescendingly. "I certainly wouldn't expect you to waste your time on a jerk.''

"Oh, Adam, loosen up and come sit down,'' she ordered, not unlike an impatient mother chastising a fractious child. And yet, while her tone held weariness, her gleaming eyes betrayed an inner merriment.

Damned if the woman didn't have the temerity to laugh at him, albeit silently, Adam railed, trying to whip himself into an indignant anger.

He failed. Instead of annoyance, his sense of fair play and amusement rose to the fore. "Okay, so I'm an uptight jerk,'' he said, his smile sheepish as he returned to the settee to drop onto it. "It's just that…this whole situation is beginning to get to me.''

"I know it's hard to accept, but…''

"Hard?'' he interjected. "Try impossible.'' He raised his hands, then let them fall onto his thighs in a gesture of helplessness. "Sunny, this concept you're asking me to buy into is straight out of the pages of New Age fiction.''

"And you're convinced all of it is fiction.''

Although she hadn't posed it as a question, Adam answered it anyway, and with a resounding, "Yes.''

She smiled, appearing not in the least put off by his adamant tone. "Well, I see I have my work cut out for me.'' She shrugged. "But then, I really never expected it to be a walk-through.'' Her smile turned wry. "I guess I was kind of hoping that by now you would have had some memory flashes, enough at any rate to give you pause for consideration."

The gunsmith's shop and his reaction to its location immediately sprang to Adam's mind. He dismissed it as irrelevant, telling himself that he had more than likely overheard someone mention the fact and unconsciously absorbed it, possibly while he was having lunch.

Yes, he assured himself, that made sense, a whole helluva lot more sense than memory flashes.

"Memory flashes," he repeated, shaking his head in despair of her. "Sunny, there are no memory flashes of past lives in the world of reality. I suggest that the stories you've related to me are elaborate, detailed fantasies, whole cloth woven from your fertile and vivid imagination."

"So there. Take that," Sunny derided, making a face at him. "Fantasies, huh?" She arched an eyebrow. "Even the dull and boring ones."

"Well...er..." Adam scoured his mind for a sensible explanation. His mind refused to cooperate, frustrating him, but it didn't matter, she wasn't waiting for one.

"And detailed? Who said they were detailed? Not I," she maintained. "I mentioned flashes, if you recall? And you should—I mentioned them often enough."

"Yes, but..." he began, without a clue as to an effective rebuttal. But again, she forged ahead.

"Your argument is insulting."

Her charge jolted him upright. "Insulting? In what way?" he demanded.

"By your assumption that I am not intelligent enough to differentiate between deliberate romantic fantasizing and spontaneous flashes of insight."

"But I never meant..." he began, in a fence-mending tone, only to once again be interrupted, and rather rudely.

"Oh, bag it, Adam, and just listen," she ordered. "When I said flashes, I meant flashes. The memories came, flashed, always unexpectedly, in brief scenes, not in a linear start-to-finish manner, similar to a film, with a beginning and an end, like a movie produced for theaters or TV. It took me years to make any kind of sense of them, most particularly when they first started. They scared the hell out of me."

Sunny paused to take a breath, and a sip of Adam's wine. Because the remembered fear was stark in her expression, in her eyes, Adam was tempted to offer words of comfort and reassurance, but certain Sunny wasn't finished, he remained silent, offering the clasp of his hand instead.

She accepted his offer with a smile and a soft sigh. "As I grew older and began to understand and accept what was happening to me, I learned to assimilate the memories. But they were still just flashes, some quite vivid, others very dim. That's why I have difficulty with names, pinpointing precise locations.'' She stared directly into his eyes. ''But they are very real, not fantasy but memories of past lives, of our past lives together, which for some unknown and inexplicable reason I have carried over into this lifetime.''

Adam watched, as—apparently having finished—Sunny took another sip of his wine, then sank back into the corner of the settee, waiting for whatever he might have to say.

And what did he have to say? he asked himself. What in hell could he say? If it hadn't been before, it was now obvious that Sunny's belief in the nature of her memory flashes was absolute, unshakable.

Was she deluded, living in a world of her own creation?

Or was there something to her beliefs?

Coming out of the left field of his consciousness, the consideration was startling. So startling, in fact, Adam spoke without thinking.

''How does this reincarnation thing work?''

''Oh, Adam, I don't know.'' Sunny gave him a helpless look. ''I have the insight of brief individual memories, not insight into the mysteries of the spiritual universe.''

Well, that was a help. Feeling disgruntled, dissatisfied, Adam exclaimed, ''Then how in the hell am I suppose to know, to understand?''

"Perhaps if I told you another one of our stories..." She paused, tentatively arching her eyebrows. "You never know, it might just jog something in your subconscious."

Then, again, it just might not, Adam thought.
But what the hell, it was raining and—other than
carrying Sunny off to bed, which he had no intention of doing this night—he had nothing better to
do.

Wryly musing that Scheherazade strikes again,
he nevertheless managed an encouraging smile and
a sweep of his hand in invitation. "Story on...but
without the cute long ago and far, far away rou-
tine, please."

She laughed. After the emotional tension of the
previous few minutes, the delightful sound had a
soothing, almost hypnotic effect.

He smiled in response, prompting, "Begin."

"This incarnation took place in Scotland," she
began, pausing when he winced at the word incarnation.

Although he knew why she had paused, Adam
chose not to address that particular issue and instead challenged the location. "Still in the British
isles, hmm?"

"Yes." She nodded. "Most of our sojourns on
earth were—until we discovered America, so to
speak."

"In effect, you're saying we choose our destinations, so to speak?'' he asked, unable to keep his voice completely free of a note of ridicule.

"Appears so." Sunny's smile was vague. "It's only a feeling, you understand, a pure guess, but it seems to me that free will plays a deciding role in the matter. Apparently we choose our destiny."

"Uh-huh." Adam chose not to elaborate, deciding that, rather than curiouser and curiouser, this encounter with Sunny was getting weirder and weirder. "And this time around—" had he actually said that? "—we chose Scotland."

She nodded. "The border."

Here it comes, he thought.

"You were what was referred to as a border lord."

He was right.

"And you were...?'' he asked, suppressing a sigh.

"The beloved daughter of a peer of the British realm," she answered, unsurprisingly.

What else? Adam reflected, idly wondering what the title might be of the historical bodice ripper she had obviously been reading prior to those memory flashes.

"You kidnapped me and held me for ransom."

Of course. The plot was formulaic, wasn't it? Scotland. Border lord. A British peer with a daughter—preferably beautiful and fiery. A kidnapping. All the elements necessary for a satisfying read. Save one.

"And we fell in love," he said, voicing the last, most important fictional element.

"On sight of one another," she concurred, validating his conviction. "But we fought our feelings—and each other—for some time."

Certainly. Adam had been expecting the plot twist. Pages had to be filled with something. Didn't they?

"Wasn't that same story on the *New York Times*'s bestseller list some years back?" he asked drolly.

Sunny seemed serenely unaffected by his mocking voice. "Could have been. If it was, I missed it." She shrugged. "But I wouldn't be surprised if it was." She returned his mockery with chiding. "There are elements of fact in fiction, and events such as I mentioned have occurred throughout recorded history…and probably before."

"I sit corrected," he drawled.

"Now who's being cute?" she retorted.

"Sorry." He meant it. "Please continue. I promise I'll keep my mouth shut."

"It'll make a change," she murmured, softening the sting with a smile. "At any rate, we were in Scotland. Or at least you were. I was traveling with my father, who from what I could discern, was making an inspection of his seldom visited properties in northern England. Along the way, we had heard many complaints from the tenants about raids being launched by the barbarians from north of the border. One name in particular was mentioned repeatedly. The name, Magnus Hunter.''

"I had a name this time?" Adam asked, unable to contain his surprise. "One you remembered?"

"Oh, yes. That one came through loud and clear." Her eyes grew bright with an unholy gleam. "But the farmers and townsfolk had their own name for you."

He should have been alerted by the devilish light in her eyes; Adam was alerted by the green brilliance, and still he played along.

"And what name was that?"

"Magnus the Head Hunter."

Nine

Adam contained a bark of laughter.

"Magnus the Head Hunter?" he asked sardonically, arching one eyebrow. "Can I assume the reference was literal, not the same as that currently used in the corporate world?"

"You can."

"Sounds formidable," he said drolly, uncertain whether he felt pleased or shamed by the designation and perplexed as to why it should bother him either way.

"Very formidable," she agreed.

"Also sounds like a Hollywood back-lot plot."

"You promised," she reminded him, and none too gently. "Are you going to listen or ridicule?"

"May I ask one more question?"

She gave him a look. "One."

"Did you have a name—one you remembered?"

"Elinor."

"Pretty."

"Yes." She raised one eyebrow. "Anything else on your mind, before I continue?"

"No. I'll be quiet now." To prove his assertion he ran the tip of a finger over his lips, as if to seal them.

"That's better," Sunny said, her expression wry. "Anyway, we had reached the most remote of my father's lands and took up residence in the castle—the smallest of all he possessed—nearby, by a small village."

"Castles?" Adam couldn't keep from remarking. "I am duly impressed."

"No, you're not," she retorted, pleasantly. "Now, please, shut up."

He refrained from further comment.

She continued. "It was my own fault that I was kidnapped. I should have known better..." A philosophical smile tilted the corners of her lips. "Perhaps I did, subconsciously."

This time Adam couldn't hold his response in check. "I don't understand. How were you at fault?"

"Despite all the warnings relayed to my father

as we traveled north, I left the castle in secret—
unattended and unguarded,'' she answered.

"So what, and why?"

She scowled at him, then went on to explain.
"It was the time of the annual local fair, and although the people of the area had obvious trepi-
dations, they agreed to hold the fair, in spite of the
reports they had received from visitors, itinerant
wanderers and traveling tinkerers, all with tales of
the rash of raiding and ravishing.''

Ravishings, yet. Though Adam was sorely
tempted to repeat the thought, yet mindful of her
warning scowl, he kept it inside his head.

"I was young, willful and defiant.'' A reminis-
cent smile curved her mouth. "I was also adven-
turous. Against my father's orders, I outwitted my
attendants and guards and stole from the castle,
determined to mingle with the peasantry and enjoy
the excitement and merriment.''

"And was it merry?"

She leveled a sparkling look at him. "You and
your men struck just as I was about to return to
the castle, creating mayhem where frivolity had
prevailed. Like the others, I ran, seeking shelter, a
sanctuary.''

Adam was struck by a sense of urgency; nothing
could have kept him from asking, "Did you find
it?"

Sunny pondered the question for a moment before responding. "Well...yes and no.''

"Huh?" He frowned.

"The no part is that I was swept off my feet by a hard-muscled arm and cruelly slammed face-down across a saddle in front of a rider, who turned out to be you."

Adam squirmed inside, but not because of her accusation. Her words had drawn a picture so vivid he felt he was actually witnessing the chaotic scene; he could smell the swirling dust mingled with the scent of food and sweating horses and men. He could hear the screams of fear from the scattering people, the battle cries from the throats of the raiders. He could see the colors of the clothing worn by the populace, the gold-streaked mane of the lone woman, fleeing in the direction of the castle in the distance.

Magnus knew who she was and that he had to have her.

The certainty of the inner knowledge startled Adam into the awareness of Sunny's voice, going on with her story.

"And just as I was beginning to fear the awful jouncing, bone-bruising ride would never end, the horse clattered into a courtyard and came to a sudden, jarring stop."

She paused to wet her lips with the tip of her tongue; without a second thought, Adam picked up his glass and held it out to her.

"Thanks," she murmured before taking a deep swallow. "I am rather dry."

"You're welcome. Can I get you a glass of white wine?" he asked, knowing she preferred it over the red.

"Hmm...no." She shook her head. "But I could drink something cold. Are there any soft drinks?"

"Sure." Adam was up and moving as he answered. Opening the door of the small cabinet, he peered inside. "There's club soda and cola, diet and regular."

"Cola, regular, please," she said, quickly adding, "in a glass with ice, if there is any."

"Of course." Making swift work of the minor chore, Adam dropped several cubes into one of the stemmed glasses, then poured the cola over them. Carrying the glass and still half-full can back to her, he handed them to her, then resettled on the settee. Feeling oddly anxious to hear the rest of her story, he waited with enforced patience.

Offering him a smile in thanks, Sunny raised the glass to her lips and took a deep swallow.

Adam was forced to swallow in reaction to the sudden dryness in his throat. The sight of her, greedily gulping the liquid had caused a twist of arousal in the most vulnerable part of his body. Bizarre in the extreme, he chided himself.

"Oh, I needed that," Sunny said, laughing a little self-consciously.

Adam clamped a lid on the urge to tell her what he needed. Pitching his voice to a low, languid drawl, to conceal his avid interest in her story, he encouraged her to continue. "You left off with the horse coming to a halt in a courtyard."

"Yes," she said, glancing up from the glass she had busied herself refilling. "My relief at the cessation of motion was short-lived, however, as my captor immediately dismounted, grabbed me and tossed me over his shoulder."

"The cad," he drawled, secretly appalled by a sensation of weight pressing down on his right shoulder. The power of suggestion, he assured himself. Still, he felt grateful when the sound of her voice once again distracted him from his unpalatable introspection.

"I put up a good fight, though," she said, her eyes dancing with an impish light.

"Did you?" Adam had no choice, he had to laugh at the sound of satisfaction in her voice.

"Damned straight. I fought like a blasted wildcat." She smirked. "That's what you...he, Magnus the Head Hunter, himself, called me. A blasted wildcat."

"And what did you call me..." Adam shook his head, swore to himself. *"Him."*

A slow, taunting smile curved her lips. Her green eyes gleamed with mockery. "A bloody bastard."

"Tsk, tsk." He frowned. "And you a proper lady."

She shrugged. "Turned out, I quickly learned I

wasn't much of a lady...and the last thing from proper.''

''Really? How did you gain this self-knowledge?'' He asked, arching his brows, even though he knew, somehow, the method of her supposed downfall.

''You seduced me.''

''Would I do that?'' Adam was uncomfortably aware of having assumed the character of Magnus; he was even more uncomfortably aware of how well the role fit him.

''Eagerly, avidly, repeatedly,'' she said, flashing a grin at him. ''You absolutely wallowed in it.''

Yes, he had, and he ached to wallow again.

The mental response rattled Adam, even as the desire to repeat the performance set fire to his senses.

''I loved it.''

Adam burst into laughter at the note of smug complacency in her tone. ''So,'' he said, controlling his laughter, ''we're back to the assumed position again.''

''Why not?'' Sunny executed a shrug that was both elegant and careless. ''We shared many delightful hours, during many lifetimes, in that position.''

''Temptress,'' he muttered, gritting his teeth against the growing urge to throw control and caution to the wind.

''I do my best,'' she admitted, taunting his reticence. "But I must confess," she went on, sighing, "you always possessed the stronger character."

"A prince among men, hmm?" he asked with wry amusement, marveling at himself for accepting first person, center stage in her imaginary play.

"A god," she simpered, ruining the effect with her flashing smile and sparkling eyes.

"Oh, get on with the story," he groaned, certain that if he didn't distract her—and himself—he'd give in to the temptation to toss her over his shoulder and carry her to bed...in exactly the same manner of Magnus the Head Hunter.

"Oh, there's not much more," Sunny said, shrugging. "If you recall, I did tell you there were only flashes of memories, little very detailed."

"How could I forget?" he shot back at her. "The word *flashes* is etched in stone in my mind."

"Good." Sunny compressed her twitching lips. "At any rate, my noble father arrived on the scene with a full compliment of men prepared to, in his exact words, which came through loud and clear in the flashes, "Wipe out this thieving nest of vipers and jackals." The twitch won, she grinned.

"And he succeeded?" Adam asked, although he knew, deep down, that he hadn't.

She shook her head. "No, the clash of swords never occurred, because you had checkmated him."

"How?" Adam was fully aware of holding his breath.

"By making me your bride, of course."

"Why would I do that?" Adam gave an impatient shake of his head. "Why would the ruthless Magnus the Head Hunter do that? I mean...why buy the cow when you've had the milk for nothing, and from an enemy English, at that?"

Sunny's expression was superior. "He—you—loved me above all else. That's why."

And he...I still do.

The sudden thought, the certainty of it, shook Adam, undermining his core beliefs.

Dammit, he railed in silent frustration. This woman, this Scheherazade of story telling, had him mentally running in circles. And, damn it to hell, he didn't believe in the concept of reincarnation.

"You must be fantastic in bed," he drawled, defending his position with crude sarcasm.

Sunny went rigid for an instant. Then she smiled, as if comprehending his motivation.

Watching her, Adam cringed inside for slinging the insult at her; she had done nothing to earn his contempt.

She was quiet for long seconds, her eyes distant, with a faraway look.

Adam instinctively knew that Sunny was looking through her avowed memories, not unlike the way in which one would look through a lifetime of snapshots in a photo album. He was about to speak, to break her trance, when her changing expression stole his breath.

Her features softened. A flush pinked her cheeks. Her lips, suddenly appearing fuller, slightly parted. The distant, faraway look in her eyes fled before the gathering clouds of smoky-green sensuousness.

"We were fantastic in bed together," she murmured, her heated gaze caressing his form and face before rising to impact on his riveted stare.

That did it. His resistance vanquished by the expanding power of his libido, Adam consigned control, caution and common sense to hell and gone.

"Sunny." Whispering her name, he moved across the settee to her...and into the arms she lifted to enfold him.

"Yes." Her answering whisper added fuel to the flames licking his system into a blaze. "Anything, everything you want, my love. I've waited so long, needed you so badly. It seems like forever."

Yes. Forever. Adam was barely aware of his subconscious, echoing her desire-roughened voice. But his consciousness was aware, painfully aware of the passion feeding his strength, burgeoning his arousal.

He had to have her, make her his again, reassert his claim of exclusivity to her.

The thought was hazy, unclear in the desire-clouded cells of his brain. The only part that made sense to Adam was the relentless drive of his need to be one with her.

Without care or gentleness, he crushed her mouth with his and speared his tongue between her parted lips.

Moaning, Sunny curled her fingers into his hair, raked her nails against his scalp, urging him closer. Her mouth clinging to his, she slid her tongue along his, greedily stoking the fire consuming him.

They were wearing too many clothes.

As if simultaneously reaching the same conclusion, they began tearing at one another's garments, the frenzy of their movements sent them toppling over the side of the settee and into a heap on the carpeted floor.

"Dammit," Adam growled, pulling back from her entangling arms and legs. "Are you hurt?"

"Just my dignity," Sunny assured him, between laughing gasps of breath.

Adam grimaced at her as he scrambled to stand. "Settees were not built for sexual calisthenics," he muttered, reaching down to help her up.

With fluid grace she came off the floor and into his arms, her body molding to his like water to an angular shoreline. A tiny section of Adam's mangled mind that had begun to function immediately shut down again.

His mouth sought hers, then holding her captive

with his lips and tongue, he moved unerringly toward the bedroom. Their hands busy, they discarded articles of each other's clothing along the way.

When they came to a halt beside the bed, they were both as nature had made them, free of the trappings of civilization and all inhibition.

As one, they tossed back the covers and fell onto the bed, immediately reaching, one for the other.

Slowly, drawing out their pleasure of tactile exploration to an excruciating, near painful arousal, they stroked, licked, caressed, probed each other and the depths of their desire and endurance.

"Do you like that?" Adam murmured, savoring the thrill of sensation as his lips again drew on the hard tip of her small but beautiful breast.

"Does this please you?" she countered in a throaty whisper, stopping his breath with the feather-light glide of her fingers along the throbbing length of his manhood.

Please him? Adam thought in a haze of desire, shivering in reaction to her caress. He wasn't sure how long he could stand, or survive the pleasure. And yet he held back from the final intimacy, his muscles clenched to impose control. There were a few pleasures yet to be derived before attaining the ultimate reward of joining with her.

Nipping, licking, then suckling at her breasts, Adam skimmed his hand up the silky length of her inner thigh to the nest of curls guarding her femininity. He dipped a finger, testing the waters of her readiness. His stomach muscles clenched when she gasped and arched into his caress.

His heart racing, his breaths shallow, he continued to pleasure her while, bestowing a final kiss on her breast, he slid his passion-slick body down hers, gliding his tongue over her midriff, her belly, the springy curls covering her mound before offering the ultimate kiss of intimacy and tasting the honey of her desire.

Sunny's body jerked and she cried out, begging him to stop, begging him for more, begging him to end the unbearable tension of her pleasure.

Her hands gripped his head and she arched into him, into the torturing pleasure of his hungry mouth. And then she went wild, rigid, sobbing with the ecstasy of the release he could feel and taste cascading through her.

Before the tremors stopped, Adam was rising to his knees, positioning himself between her thighs and then plunging into the moist depths of her climax.

He was home.

The thought didn't register.

Every muscle in his body taut with readiness, Adam took his own pleasure, driving into the slick, satiny sheath with single-minded purpose. He felt, thrilled, to her quickening response. And then they

were moving together, one being seeking the apex
of mutual fulfillment.

Teeth clenched, he held on, to Sunny and to his
control, until he felt the first faint tremors move
through her. Casting off restraint, he increased his
effort, plunging once, twice more into her. He
heard her cry out his name an instant before he
exploded into an ecstatic release, his echoing cry
bursting from his tight throat.

"Sunny."

Ten

Adam lay on his back, Sunny held tightly to his still quivering body; one hand idly stroking over her hip and thigh, Adam's mind in a state of stunned shock in response to the most unbelievably beautiful experience he had ever lived through and survived.

Or had he survived? he mused fancifully; maybe he had died and gone to heaven. For being with Sunny, inside her, one with her, had been as close to heaven as he dared hope to get...at least in this lifetime.

This lifetime? Now where had that idea sprung from? Adam asked himself. Shifting position in reaction to a sudden chill along his spine, he absently tightened his arms around Sunny's soft sleeping form.

Sunny. His body quickened at the mere thought of her name. She was magnificent while in the throes of unleashed passion; wild in response to his every caress.

He had been lying quiet while his racing heartbeat decreased to a more normal level and his harsh, shallow breaths grew less labored, but recalling their spectacular union reignited his senses, rearoused his libido.

He wanted her again, that quickly he felt desperate to be sheathed within her, experience that shattering, multicolored moment of sheer bliss.

But Sunny slept and he didn't have the heart to...

She stirred, innocently sliding one silky thigh between his legs, tearing a ragged breath from his chest with an unconscious brush of her knee against his sex.

Adam's teeth snapped together while his hormones fell apart. He held his breath, pitting his will against the rioting demands of his hardening body.

Sunny sighed, and wedged her knee into the juncture of his thighs. Beads of sweat broke out on his forehead and above his upper lip. His will betrayed him, surrendering to his body's raging need to possess her, own her, literally stake his claim to this woman...*his* woman.

The compelling desire was so all-consuming it was near frightening. Never, never had Adam lusted so completely, so atavistically for a woman, any woman. Never before had he been motivated by the force of his sexual appetite.

But this woman, Sunny, was different. Being with her, one with her, was like being reunited with a missing part of himself, making him feel whole, complete.

Adam was trembling from the inner battle he was waging against an invasion of her sleeping body, when Sunny woke up and saved him from self-degradation.

"I want you again," she murmured with guileless honesty, leaving a trail of fire on his collarbone with the brush of her lips. "Is it too soon for you?"

Too soon? She offered to save his sanity and asks if it's too soon? Adam marveled, unsure whether to laugh exultantly or cry in abject relief.

"Er, no, it's not too…" He broke off, sucking in a breath at the feel of her fingers curling around him.

"So I can feel," she purred, intensifying the thrill with a quick stab of her tongue into the hollow at the base of his taut throat.

Adam wanted to go slow with her this time, draw out each new and exciting sensation; he wanted to, but he couldn't. Not only would his body not cooperate, Sunny would not allow him to proceed at a more leisurely pace.

She was like a tigress, voracious in her hunger for him. Seizing the initiative, she made love to him, driving him mad with her biting kisses, her playful tongue and her busy, skillful hands.

Adam was a goner. He knew it and he loved it, every erotic, mind-blowing minute of it.

She mounted him. Thrilling to her possession of him, he arched into her in willing surrender. Caressing him, murmuring words of enticement, she rode him into an explosive shower of shimmering ecstasy.

Completely undone by the intensity of their union, Adam fell into a deep sleep, Sunny's spent body sprawled atop his, his body still joined to hers.

"Cold."

Sunny's sleep-furred voice woke Adam a few hours before dawn. She was still asleep, and trembling. Chagrined by his precipitous capitulation to slumber, he gently disengaged from her and lifted her from him.

The movement, or absence of warmth, or both, woke her. Blinking, she gazed at him in puzzlement.

"I want to put us under the covers," he explained, sitting up and reaching for the bed covers they had somehow managed to kick to the floor during their exertions.

"What time is it?"

Adam shot a glance at the clock on the nightstand. "Almost four." Grasping the edge of the bedclothes, he dragged them up and over her shivering form. "What time must you get back to your place to get ready for work?"

"By seven-thirty," she answered, raising a hand to her mouth to smother a yawn. "Oh, this feels better," she murmured, snuggling under the covers.

Picking up the receiver on the bedside phone, Adam placed a wake-up call for six forty-five, then slid beneath the covers next to her. Drawing her into his arms, he settled her warming body close to his own.

"Go back to sleep," he whispered, unnecessarily; Sunny was already out like a light.

It quickly became evident to Adam that he wouldn't be able to follow his own advice. Sleep eluded him. With Sunny's head nestled into the curve of his shoulder, he inhaled the fresh, herbal-shampoo scent of her hair.

He could fall in love with her. He might even already be in love with her. Never having experienced the emotion, Adam had no yardstick with which to measure the breadth and depth of his feelings.

Adam sighed. He had heard and been assured

of the very real possibility of love at first sight.
Then again, he had always heard that falling in
love made people feel wonderful. He didn't feel
wonderful. Oh, physically he felt joyous, replete,
utterly satisfied, at least for the moment, he conceded to himself. The loving had exceeded expectations.

But.

Adam grimaced. There always seemed to be a
but, he thought, a but or a what-if or an if-only.

In his case, the three combined into one over-
riding cautioning question.

Sunny believed without a single doubt that they
had shared previous lifetimes.

Adam didn't share her beliefs…despite the moment of confused uncertainty concerning the gunsmith's shop.

So, then, how was he to proceed? he asked himself, drawing her shampoo-female scent deep into
his lungs. In love with her, or merely on the brink
of loving her, Adam wanted to be with her, and
not just for a brief, romantic holiday affair. He
wanted her with him, by his side. He felt so at-
tuned to her that even after their brief acquaintance
of only two days, he was certain of his intentions.

He would eventually want marriage, a joining
of their lives as well as their bodies, a true partnership opposed to a now-and-then, hit-or-miss relationship.

But could a true partnership between them endure, survive the strain of their opposing beliefs?

And therein lay the but that bit, the what-if they couldn't agree to disagree on, the if-only she wasn't so adamant about, convincing him her beliefs were true.

Adam couldn't imagine himself ever accepting the concept of reincarnation, never mind Sunny's claim that they continued to reincarnate to be together. While he would be willing to grant that the theory was romantic, it conflicted greatly with his logical, rational way of thinking.

And where a conflict existed, a conflict not merely of different interests but a serious conflict of core beliefs, could a relationship endure?

Adam was very much afraid that the answer was no. In his casual observation of the marriages and liaisons of friends and relatives, he could not have avoided noticing the difficulties inherent in maintaining a relationship, even when there appeared to be little conflict. By its very nature, a romantic relationship demanded compromises between two diverse and very different personalities.

But could he compromise his core beliefs?

Adam knew that he could not.

So where did that leave him? he asked himself.

Knowing the answer, yet unwilling to face it, his arms tightened convulsively around Sunny's pliant form.

He couldn't stand the thought of parting from her, losing her, but...

"What are you thinking?" Her quiet voice intruded into his troubling introspection.

"That I'm tired." It was the first and only response he could dredge from his weary mind. The fact that it was true was irrelevant. "I'm sorry if I woke you," he went on, in a deliberate attempt to change the subject.

"Oh, that's all right," she said, peering at the bedside clock. "It's almost time to get up, anyway." She shifted her expressive eyes to his; laughter lurked in their green depths. "Besides, if I'm going to be crushed, I'd as soon it be in your embrace."

Adam loosened his hold at once, although he didn't release her. "I'm sorry. I..."

"Adam," she interrupted.

"Yes?"

"Shut up and kiss me good-morning."

Shoving his bleak outlook for their future to the back of his mind, Adam quickly complied, losing his concerns in the sweet and hot forgetfulness of her mouth.

They shared a shower, and each other, and then he reluctantly drove her home.

After no sleep at all the night before, and only a brief nap earlier, in addition to his physical endeavors and subsequent wearying mental activity, followed by more physical endeavor, Adam felt exhausted and it showed.

"Go back to your room and get some sleep," Sunny advised in a murmur, lightly stroking her fingertips over the shadows beneath his eyes.

"I plan to," he assured her, catching her hand and drawing it to his lips to kiss her fingers. "Sunny, about this evening…" he hesitantly began, torn between his desire to see her, be with her, and an equally compelling belief that he needed some breathing space, thinking time away from the distraction of her company.

"I've rattled you, haven't I?" she asked, as if she had read his thoughts and emotions.

"Yes." Adam was nothing if not honest and forthright. "You must admit it all sounds a little weird."

"And you're having trouble dealing with it." Since it wasn't a question, she didn't wait for a reply but continued on, "I expected you would."

"Then, you don't mind if…"

"Of course, I mind," she interrupted. "I mind like the very devil." Leaning into him, she kissed his receptive mouth, hard. "But I do understand," she assured him, sighing as she withdrew. She reached for the door release and pushed open the door.

"I'll call you in a day or so," he said, feeling slightly sick and missing her already.

"Maybe," she said, her eyes sad. "It's all true, you know. Everything I've told you is true."

The feeling of sickness expanded inside Adam. "I know you believe that, but..." his voice faded and he moved his shoulders in a helpless, hopeless shrug.

"You can't or won't believe it," she finished for him, despair weighing her tone. "And unless you can accept it, you can't accept me."

He didn't respond, didn't know how to respond.

Sunny stepped out of the car.

"Sunny." Her name burst from his throat in a hoarse, whispered cry.

She shook her head and moved away from the car.

Though Adam felt like something was clawing him apart inside, he let her go.

Eleven

He was searching, searching, looking for signs of the passage of his tribe. He had to find them, find her, his woman, his mate.

He was no longer naked; the blue paint was gone. His hips and loins were girdled, swathed by the short leather skirt of a Roman foot soldier. Leather sandals encased his feet. His right hand gripped the hilt of a Roman short sword.

He did not concern himself with pursuit; his Roman captor had bid him go, find his mate. Then, if his belief in the One True God proved constant, abiding, he could return, with or without his life mate.

He knew he would return. He had no choice.

Enthralled by the teachings of the mission of the man called Jesus of Galilee and the One True God, he thirsted for more, to feel as one with this Supreme Being.

But he needed his mate by his side.

Sharp anxiety twisted within him, a sense of urgency so strong he felt he dare not stop searching—not to eat, not to sleep, not to rest. He had to find them, his people; he had to find her.

There had been women at the Roman encampment, lovely women, pampered women, willing women, eager to test the strength and power of the savage Celt.

His lip curled and he made a harsh, snarling sound deep in his throat.

Those women held no appeal for him, with their filmy garments and perfumed skin.

His body ached for, his mind cried out for, his soul—the wondrous soul the priests had told him he possessed—yearned for her, his life mate, his woman.

Blessed relief surged through him at the unmistakable markings of the passing.

He arrived at the new, hastily constructed settlement late in the day. He knew at once that something was amiss. Dread filling him, he followed the sounds of grief.

He found her in her parents' dwelling. Horror smote him at the sight of her broken body, the contractions of her distended belly, the anguish twisting her beloved face.

Flinging others aside, he made his way to her, dropping to his knees beside her crude pallet.

She was dying.

Grasping her slender hand, he bowed his head, unmindful of the tears streaming down his sweat-streaked face.

Holy Mother of God, he prayed to the Blessed Virgin, have mercy. If it can be accomplished, intercede with your Son for her life. If not, take this heathen woman into your most compassionate care.

In an agony of grief and remorse, he made a vow to her. Swearing his love for her, and in the belief of the Man who had taught of life everlasting, he promised her that they would be together again, throughout eternity.

She died with his name on her lips.

The sword of inconsolable grief pierced his heart, rendered his mind.

Screaming his pain, he ran and ran...

The sound of his hoarse cry woke Adam from the nightmare. Gasping for breath, he jolted upright in the bed, wild eyes skimming over the shadowy room.

There were no trees, no forest, no cold, lifeless body of his beloved.

Sunny. The woman writhing in agony, her dis-

tended belly contracting in labor to expel the dead child from her body, in the dream was Sunny.

At that moment Adam was jolted into the horrifying realization of his failure to use any form of protection for Sunny or himself during their lovemaking.

How could he have forgotten? He never forgot. And yet with her he had forgotten, thus put her at risk.

Shuddering, Adam blinked and focused on his surroundings, searching for...

There was only the motel room, the midday light blocked by the drawn drapes.

Adam was shivering, and yet his body was slick with sweat. Raising a shaky hand, he drew it over his face, startled to discover his tears mingled with perspiration.

It was only a dream, he told himself, a reenactment by his imagination of the story Sunny had told him.

But it had seemed so real. He had felt the anxiety, the sense of urgency...and then the terrible thrust of pain, the bitter taste of loss.

Adam knew he could not bear to live through a similar situation. Before he left Virginia, he would have to contact Sunny, assure her he would take full responsibility if she had conceived his child.

The chances of him having impregnated her probably were slim, but if it had occurred, he wanted her to know he would not attempt to shirk his responsibility.

And yet, common sense told him the odds were in his, their favor. In all likelihood, he was worrying for nothing.

Tossing the tangled covers from him, he shifted to sit on the edge of the bed, noting the dampness of the sheets where he had lain.

Heaving a sigh, he glanced at the clock. The digits read 1:27 p.m. It had been after eight when he had crawled into bed; he had slept less than five and a half hours.

Adam considered lying down and trying to go back to sleep. But the sheet was damp, and though he felt even more exhausted than before he'd slept, he was wide-awake, and in truth he was afraid he'd fall back into the nightmare.

Deciding he needed a shower, food, and then some brisk exercise in the bracing, fresh December air, somewhere removed from the restored area with its constant reminders of the past, he headed for the bathroom.

It was much colder in the Blue Ridge Mountains. Though the rain of the day before had abated sometime during the morning while Adam was sleeping, the sky remained overcast, the air moist and biting, more what Adam was accustomed to in the mountains of Wyoming.

Of course, the Blue Ridge Mountains, as part of

the long Appalachian range, were different from the Rockies. They weren't nearly as high or rocky. There were more trees, a lot more trees.

Adam noted the differences whenever he took a fancy to pull the car into a scenic-view area, and along every walking trail he wandered for a half mile or so.

He drew deep breaths of cold air into his lungs, enjoying the scent of moisture-laden fir and pine, and tried to imagine how it would smell in the dryer summer months.

He lingered in the mountains until dusk, then headed back to Williamsburg and the motel, driving well within the posted speed limit. He stopped to eat at a roadside restaurant, enjoying both the meal and the soft Virginia drawl in the voices of his fellow dining patrons.

It was late when he arrived back at the motel and he was tired, physically and mentally. But the excursion had had the desired effect; the sense of anxiety and confusion he had awakened with were gone. He felt a lot better than when he started out. His equilibrium had been restored.

The excursion had been what he'd needed, Adam decided, crawling into the freshly made bed after a relaxing hot shower. Distancing himself from the trappings of the past and from the reason-testing claims made by Sunny, had realigned his normal, logical perspective.

Despite the dictates of his body and emotions to

seek out Sunny, continue their mind- and senses-blowing affair, Adam advised himself to keep his distance.

He could function much more efficiently without soul-wrenching dreams such as the shattering one he had experienced that morning.

His course set to his rational bent, if not his inner satisfaction, Adam fell asleep. If there were dreams, he didn't remember them upon waking.

Reinvigorated by the nine hours of deep, uninterrupted slumber, he felt energetic and prepared to face another foray into the restored area and the past.

But first things first, he told himself, exiting the suite; and the first thing on his mind was to fill his empty stomach with a good southern breakfast.

Maybe he'd even try grits, Adam thought as he strode from the elevator. He was approaching the restaurant when the vaguely familiar face of the man walking toward him caught his attention and arrested his progress.

"Good morning," the elderly gentleman called, offering his hand and a smile.

The familiar sound of the man's voice, his smile and the twinkle in his eyes, activated Adam's memory.

"Mr. White, isn't it?" he asked, smiling as he accepted the man's handshake.

"That's the role I play." He chuckled. "My real name is Lawrence, Charles Lawrence."

"Grainger, Adam," Adam supplied, grinning. "I didn't recognize you at first in modern attire."

Charles Lawrence grinned back at him. "I don't start work until later. I had an errand to run this morning and decided it would be better to do it in my regular clothes. I don't get stopped and queried that way." The twinkle in his eyes grew brighter. "While I love my work, there are times when I appreciate being just another face in the crowd."

"I can imagine," Adam responded, laughing. He hesitated, then acting on impulse, proffered an invitation. "I was about to go into the restaurant for breakfast. Would you care to join me for a meal—or just a cup of coffee?"

"Since breakfast was my intent, as well," Charles Lawrence replied, "I'd be delighted."

It wasn't until they were seated and the server had taken their breakfast orders that Charles Lawrence threw a verbal curveball that rattled Adam.

"I'd remark upon the coincidence that brought us to meet this morning," he said, his eyes fairly dancing with inner amusement. "But I don't believe in coincidence."

"No?" Adam raised his eyebrows, while feeling his spirits sink. "Why not?"

"I've learned better."

"How?" Adam asked, frowning. "I mean, how could you, anyone, possibly know differently?"

"Through experience, Mr. Grainger."

"Adam, please," he said, his frown deepening. "And I'm afraid I don't understand, Mr. Lawrence."

"Charles, please," he reciprocated, his smile indulgent. "You see, Adam, I know that it is certainly not coincidental that I am here, in this particular location, at this particular point." He paused to take a tentative sip of the steaming coffee the waiter had served them.

"You're referring to the restored area?" Adam took the opportunity to clarify.

"Precisely." Charles's nod was emphatic. "If you'll allow me to give you a brief personal history?"

Taking a deep swallow of his coffee—because now he really needed a shot of caffeine—Adam responded with a brief nod of agreement.

"I'm originally from upstate New York, a small town you've probably never heard of," Charles tacked on, smiling. "I was a teacher by profession...a history teacher."

His eyes took on a faraway look—an expression that by now Adam had become accustomed to seeing in Sunny's eyes. Steeling himself against an eerie sensation invading him, he murmured, "Go on, please."

Charles blinked, then smiled. "Yes, of course. I'm sorry for wandering off, but it still amazes me."

"What does?" Adam prompted, sparing a smile

of thanks for the waiter as he served their breakfasts.

Charles likewise smiled at the waiter and tasted his scrambled eggs before continuing with his account. "I always felt a particular interest in American history, especially the prerevolution period. Do you like the grits?"

Startled by the sudden switch in subject, Adam laughed and admitted, "No."

"Can't say I do, either," Charles said, laughing with him. "Must be an acquired taste. Now, where was I?"

"Your interest in prerevolution history," Adam reminded him.

"Ah, yes." Charles nodded, finished chewing and swallowed before continuing. "My wife and I often talked about visiting Colonial Williamsburg, but with having to raise and educate four children, we never could find the time—" he grinned "—not to mention the money. After our youngest finished college and was on his own, we started saving and planning. We came down here the spring after I retired." An odd expression crossed his face. "It was strange, but from the minute we arrived I felt as if I belonged here."

"Belonged?" Adam asked. "In what way?"

"Like I had at long last come home. After discussing with my wife the feasibility of relocating, I applied for a job, and was accepted, as a part-time reenactor. We subsequently sold our house in

New York and bought another small place here. I have never regretted it.'' Finishing the last of his meal, Charles sat back in his chair.

Adam stared at his own empty plate in consternation; he couldn't recall tasting any of his food. The resumption of Charles's recollections snared his attention.

''In the beginning, when I was experiencing sharp and clear moments of déjà vu, I was shocked by a seeming familiarity of places, things and people....'' He smiled. ''Not living people, you understand, but people famous and anonymous, long since gone. And the really startling, almost frightening thing was, I saw myself as one of them, living with them.''

''You're referring to reincarnation,'' Adam said, stifling a sigh of resignation.

''Yes.'' Charles arched his brows. ''I take it you don't believe in reincarnation.''

''No.'' He shrugged. ''I believe in the here and now, in logic and reality.''

''So did I,'' Charles assured him. ''In fact, I was a critical skeptic of anything paranormal.''

''But being here, in this restored area, made a believer out of you?'' Adam asked, wryly.

''Over time,'' Charles admitted. ''And after some rather thorough research.''

''Research?'' Adam frowned. ''How did you go about gathering research on something like that?''

"By visiting the museum of the sleeping prophet."

"The who?" Adam exclaimed.

"Edgar Cayce Museum in Virginia Beach."

The name rang a distant bell in Adam's mind; he had heard the name before, but... He shook his head.

"They called him the sleeping prophet, because he diagnosed illnesses and made predictions about the future while in a trance state," Charles explained.

"Diagnosed?" Adam asked. "For whom?"

"Many, many people," Charles said. "From thousands of miles away. People he had never seen, would never see. His diagnoses and prescribed treatment proved effective in most instances."

Adam looked skeptical.

"It's documented." Charles smiled. "He also recounted his own previous life memories. What I learned there, in addition to what I experienced here, made a believer of me."

Adam didn't respond. What was there to say?

"And so, Adam, that is why I don't believe in coincidence," Charles went on, bringing his explanation full circle. "I couldn't convince myself that it was a coincidence, pure chance, that brought me here at the exact moment in my life when I was ready, open for a complete change in my life."

"Well..." Adam shrugged. "Things happen," he said—inadequately, he knew.

"But that's my point," Charles countered. "Things don't just happen, willy-nilly, without purpose or design. I feel certain my encounter with you today, at this precise time, was not a coincidence, either."

"But..." Adam shook his head, and laughed—a bit uneasily. "What could be the purpose or design of our meeting in the lobby of a motel?"

Charles smiled; his expression was both encouraging and compassionate. "Since I know why I'm here, I suggest you will have to work the answer to that one out by yourself."

It was late when Adam returned to the motel from Virginia Beach. In spite of his reservations, and the certainty he was on a wild-goose chase, he had driven to the beach resort town soon after parting company with Charles Lawrence.

Adam had spent hours in the museum, studying the information on display about the sleeping prophet. He had come away still unconvinced of the theory of reincarnation, but impressed by the amazing life of Edgar Cayce.

The unassuming man appeared to have lived to serve.

Incredible...and humbling.

However impressed, Adam had not been inspired to exist simply for the betterment of man-

kind. While he could admire the selflessness of
another, he knew himself to be a man of rational
self-interest.

And rational self-interest was urging Adam to
cut and run, distance himself from the unsettling
effects of the restored area in general and Sunny
in particular.

Before falling asleep Adam told himself he
would give it one more day, and he had not yet
seen the Governor's Palace and Bruton Parish
Church. He could give the remaining exhibits a
pass. Come the day after, he would be checking
out of the motel and flying home to Wyoming.

Twelve

"If you will step this way, please?" the reenactor invited. Swinging open two wide doors, the costumed young man preceded the group of tourists into the long room. "This, as you can see, is the ballroom."

Shuffling along with the crowd, Adam entered the ballroom in the Governor's Palace. It was impressive, and yet...a frown etched a line between his brows.

Good...but not quite right, he thought, giving the interior a closer inspection. As with the rest of the palace, the decorations appeared authentic...but not for the particular period mentioned by the reenactor and definitely not for that particular governor.

A spasm of unease clutched at Adam's stomach muscles.

How did he know?

The certainty he felt was exactly the same as he'd experienced at the sight of the gunsmith's shop.

Dammit! He had thought, believed he had overcome the imaginings instilled into his sensually clouded mind by Sunny and her New Age babble.

Feeling his breakfast churn, Adam was relieved to hear the guide invite them to explore the palace gardens.

The minute he was outside, he separated from the group, drawing deep breaths of the chill air. Distracted, he strolled the extensive gardens, the maze in the lower terrace. Blind to his surroundings, he didn't notice if the landscaping held true to the stated historical period.

It was that dream, following so soon after the unnerving incident concerning the gunsmith's shop, Adam assured himself, rationalizing the sensation of recognition of decor and furnishings of a period nearly one hundred years prior to the events leading up to the War of Independence.

The effects of that damn dream, the gunsmith's shop, were playing hell with his imagination.

Dismissing the odd occurrences, Adam exited the palace grounds and ambled along the road parallel the Palace Green, noting the Wythe house as he made for Bruton Parish Church on the corner.

Entering through the side into the property, he gave the churchyard cemetery a pass and strode along the walkway to the front entrance of the church.

The hushed serenity inside the church soothed his rattled nervous system. An appreciative smile for the austerity of the old church curving his lips, Adam slowly traversed the center aisle. Seemingly of their own volition, his steps came to an abrupt halt midway along the aisle.

Almost afraid to move, yet aware that he had little choice, he sliced a narrowed look to his left.

That was the pew.

In that instant, with that thought, Adam could see himself sitting in that pew. But the self he saw was not the current self, but a younger self, a man in his early twenties, tall, lanky, his face somber, attired in garb of the same period as the decor and furnishings in the palace.

A stifled feeling, claustrophobic in nature, assailed him. Turning on his heel, Adam strode at a near run from the building, onto Duke of Gloucester Street and down the two blocks to Merchant's Square.

His mind haunted by the shades of the nightmare and other strange yet familiar ghosts, Adam didn't stop to investigate the shops in Merchant's Square; he didn't even notice the shop windows, festive and gleaming with holiday decorations. As if obeying a silent yet compelling command, he kept walking, crossing the road and onto the campus of the College of William and Mary.

He had been there before, studied there…taught there. Adam shook his head at the fanciful idea… but it wouldn't be denied. The idea held firm, inexorably drawing him deeper into the campus environs.

The day was clear, the bright sunshine robbing the light breeze of the cold sting of winter.

Adam no longer noticed the weather. He was barely aware of the tourists and students laughing and conversing as they moved about on the paths.

With his inner eye, his sights caught glimpses of his younger self, aging as he strode back and forth between the college and the town of Williamsburg.

Bits and pieces of the young, then not so young man's history sprang into Adam's mind.

He had come to Williamsburg from Richmond to study at the college, already then nearly twenty years in existence. But he had not come only to further his education, but to search—he knew not for what or whom.

Upon completion of his studies, he had been offered a teaching post, an associate professorship. He had accepted the post and had lived the remainder of his life there, searching, yet never finding the object of his search. He had married, not for love but companionship. He had fathered three children, not in the throes of loving passion but in physical desire. He had died a widower at the advanced age of eighty-two.

Adam shivered as the last bit of history illuminated his consciousness.

He had gone to his grave still searching.

The emptiness was a yawning chasm inside Adam.

Damn that mind-messing dream.

Making an abrupt turn, Adam literally fled the campus, his long-legged stride eating up the short distance to the small apartment above the camera shop.

Sunny answered the door, to his eyes delectable dressed in old jeans, a faded sweatshirt with the logo Virginia Is for Lovers emblazoned across the front. Her lovely face was free of makeup, her glorious gold-streaked hair a mass of disarrayed curls tumbling over her shoulders and down her back. Her slender, elegant feet were bare.

Her expressive eyes stared at him, sadness clouding the pools of deep green.

"I had to see you," he confessed, at that moment realizing her door had been his eventual destination all along.

"But...the other day...you said..." she began, a glimmer of hope crowding the sadness in her eyes.

"I know what I said," he interrupted her, giving a light shrug of helplessness. "I've changed my mind." He hesitated, unsure of her, her welcome, before admitting, "I want to be with you. Not to take you to bed," he hastily clarified, "but to talk, just be together."

Sunny smiled, chasing the clouds from her eyes and his nightmare-haunted mind.

"Will you come with me?" he asked in imploring tones. "Have dinner with me?"

"I must change," she said, indicating her clothes with a sweep of her hand.

"You're fine as you are," he assured her, meaning it. "We can order room service sent up to the suite." He lowered his gaze, then smiled. "You might want to put on shoes."

"That was good." Sunny grinned across the small table at him. "Now that one appetite's appeased, are you sure you don't want to take me to bed?"

"Temptress," Adam scolded, grinning back at her.

"I do my best."

Adam laughed. "And your best is very good," he said, still chuckling. "Darn near perfect."

"I don't have to get up for work tomorrow," she said as an inducement. "It's my day off."

On the spot, Adam decided to forget flying back to Wyoming in the morning.

"Then there's no hurry, is there?" He could hear the winding thread of sensuality in his voice. "We have all night. Let's savor every moment."

Rising from the small table, he lifted a dark bottle from a silver ice bucket set next to the table. "More wine?"

"Yes, thank you." Sunny raised her nearly empty flute for him to refill. Her eyes gleamed with inner amusement. "Only you would order an expensive champagne with a dinner of California cheeseburgers and French fries."

Adam shrugged. "I thought the wine was an excellent compliment to our meal." Turning away, he strolled to the settee and sat down, not in the one corner this time, but in the center of the seat.

"Are you deserting me?" Sunny asked, her voice dejected, her expression woeful.

"Not likely," he drawled, and patted the cushion next to him, lifting his hand to hold it out to her. "Come on over here, Scheherazade, and tell me a story."

"Scheherazade?" Sunny murmured, arching her brows in feigned surprise. "How intriguing."

Glass in hand, she rose and crossed to him, stepping out of her shoes before curling up beside him. Draping his arm around her shoulders, Adam drew her closer, thrilling to the feel of her warm body pressing against his.

Two days, only two days had passed since last he'd been with her, and yet it had seemed like weeks. Missing her, wanting to be with her, had eaten away at him like an acid.

Adam's arm tightened convulsively in reaction

to his thoughts. Unfortunately, Sunny was in the process of taking a sip of wine at the time. The pale gold liquid spilled over the edge, bathing her lips and chin.

"Adam!" she yelped on a choked burst of laughter. "Be careful. Are you trying to drown me in wine?"

"What a way to go," he muttered, grinning as he plucked the glass from her hand, then lowered his head to lap up the spill with his tongue.

"You're crazy," she said, her breaths suddenly quick, uneven. "But I love it."

"Hmm…" Adam murmured, gliding his tongue over her wine-drenched lips. "Sunny wine. Delicious, a fine vintage," he decided, dipping his tongue into her mouth.

"A-A-Adam…" Her voice was jerky, breathy. "I…er, thought you…ah…wanted to hear… Oh!" She gasped at the nip of his teeth into her lower lip.

"Right now, all I want to hear is you asking me to take you to bed," he whispered against her mouth.

"Oh, Adam…" She sighed. "Please, take me to bed."

He reached for her, then paused, his hands grasping her upper arms.

"Adam, what is it?" She looked surprised. "Is something wrong?"

"No, everything's right," he said. "I just want you to know that this time I'll protect you."

"And if it's already too late?" she asked, her voice soft, her gaze intent.

"I'll assume full responsibility," he promised. "And I'll support you in whatever way you decide to handle it. Do you understand?"

"Yes, but it wasn't necessary for you to say it."

Her answer stirred his curiosity. "Why wasn't it? Are you saying you trust me?"

"Absolutely."

"Thank you." Leaning forward, he brushed his lips over hers. "Your trust is safe with me."

"I know." Sunny's smile illuminated the dark corners of his soul. "Now, will you please take me to bed?"

"With pleasure," he said, springing up and scooping her into his arms. "Yours and mine."

"Adam! My hair!" Sunny's yelp woke him from the depths of satiated slumber. "You're laying on my hair."

"Oh..." he grumbled, blinking the sleep from his eyes. "Sorry." Heaving a sigh, he sat up, freeing her hair.

"That hurt." Rubbing her scalp, Sunny sat up beside him. The covers folded to drape her hips.

Adam's body stirred on sight of her exposed breasts. Tamping down an urge to shield those tip-tilted globes of enticement with his hands, he sprang from the bed.

"I'm for a shower," he said, sliding a slow, sidelong, smoldering look at her. "Want to join me?"

Sunny gave him a considering look. "Do you mean that literally or figuratively, sir?"

"Both," he answered, and growled at her.

"You talked me into it." Laughing, Sunny scrambled from the bed and into his arms.

"This brings back memories of a time we bathed together in a creek," Sunny mused aloud, raising her face to the shower spray and groaning in pleasurable response to his hands lathering her breasts.

"It does, huh?" Adam said, absently, his attention centered on her puckering nipples.

"Yes," she murmured, sighing in pleasure. "Only then, the water was cold." She opened her eyes to gaze into his. "Did you know that cold water is very arousing?"

"You don't say?" he said, his tone deceptively mild as he reached around her to turn off the hot-water tap. "I feel I must test your claim."

"Yikes! Adam! That's freezing!" Sunny screeched.

"Yeah, I feel it—and see it, too." His fascinated gaze was riveted to her hard nipples. "It's having a great effect on your body."

"Hmm..." Her gaze skimmed down his torso to settle on the proof of his arousal. "Yours, too." She shivered.

"Cold?" he asked in a purr, drawing her into his arms, flattening her breasts against his chest. "Let me warm you up a bit." Cradling her bottom, he lifted her to him.

"Not cold," Sunny muttered into the curve of his shoulder. "Hot, very hot," she said, curling her legs around his hips and moaning as he slipped inside her.

"Then allow me to cool you down."

The cold water beat a steady stream over them; caught up in their heated sensuality, they didn't notice.

"Well, what do you think?"

Adam turned to look at Sunny, posed in the doorway to the bedroom, and burst out laughing. His cotton-knit sweater hung down her legs to just above the knees, and he knew that beneath the sweater all she had on was the clean pair of cotton briefs he'd tossed at her when she had voiced her distaste at putting her panties back on after their extended shower.

"You look like a little girl playing dress up with her father's clothes," he said, but then immediately shook his head to negate the statement. "No, you don't. A little girl looks innocent. You look sexy as hell."

"Oh, good. I've always wanted to look sexy as hell." Sunny sashayed to him and dropped down onto the settee next to him. "Did you order coffee?"

"Yes." Raising his hand, he caught a damp tendril of her hair and coiled it around a finger. "And a cheese-and-fruit tray to go with it."

"Fine…as long as you don't expect me to peel and feed grapes to you."

"I hadn't thought of that," he said, running a speculative glance over her. "But the idea has merit."

"Forget it."

Adam heaved a dramatic sigh. "No 'me master, you slave' games, hmm?"

"No." She laughed. "But I am willing to do the Scheherazade thing." She wiggled her eyebrows, and lowered her voice to a seductive murmur. "Wanna hear a story?"

"Sure, why…" Adam broke off at a tap on the door. "That must be room service with our coffee."

"And with me only half dressed," Sunny cried, jumping up and dashing into the bedroom.

Shaking his head and laughing to himself, Adam walked to the door and admitted the waiter.

After the soft-voiced man deposited the tray on the table, pocketed Adam's generous tip and departed, Adam called the all clear to Sunny. He was pouring out their coffees when she sauntered back into the room and flopped onto the settee.

"I heard the laughter in your voice," she said, contriving to sound affronted. "I amuse you, do I?"

"You delight me," he countered, somewhat surprised at the unvarnished truth of his statement. Carrying their cups to the settee, he handed one to her, then carefully seated himself beside her, thinking they certainly were getting his money's worth out of that particular piece of furniture...not to mention the bed.

"You make me feel good, too," he added.

Sunny inclined her head. "I live to serve and pleasure you, sir," she said meekly.

"But no grapes," he qualified.

"No grapes." She laughed. "But I'll tell you a story, if you like?"

"I like." Dipping his head, he gave her a quick kiss. "Story on, Scheherazade."

Sunny made a face at him. Then she grew serious, almost somber. "There have been lifetimes when we haven't been together, you know."

Adam felt an inner jolt, as if from an electric current. "There were?"

"Yes." She nodded. "There is one, in particular. The images were vivid in their very drabness."

Adam frowned. "I don't understand."

"I was alone, the only child of a Virginia gentleman farmer. I had been privileged, raised in what at that time was considered the lap of luxury.''

''That was drab?'' he asked, making the connection between her claim to having been in Virginia and the strange visions he had experienced on the college campus earlier.

Could it be possible they had been there at the same time, and through some quirk had never met?

The thought had no sooner flickered to life inside his head, when he dismissed it.

Ridiculous.

''My life was drab, not my living conditions,'' she explained. ''I had numerous suitors, and yet none of them suited me. I had a longing inside, a sick yearning for someone...'' Her smile was tinged with sadness. ''I longed, yearned for you.''

''And you knew it was me you longed for?'' Adam asked, a roughness edging his voice as he recalled the endless searching of the man, the self, in his visions.

''No, not then.'' Sunny sighed. ''It was only with the flash of memories that I understood what the woman who had been me had been longing for.''

Adam didn't respond; he couldn't. He was too caught up in reliving what had frighteningly appeared to be his own flashes of memory.

Then another consideration struck him. She had told him that first day that Mr. White had been here before; Adam had presumed she had meant during the present lifetime. Then Charles Lawrence had said he had been here before, with a definite indication of a previous lifetime.

Had they known one another then?

"I never married." Sunny's soft voice snagged his wandering attention. "I never knew the caress of a man, the possession of a lover. I lived out my life alone."

"But..." Adam hesitated, uneasy in his mind, silenced by the memory flash of a man searching, longing, yet not living out his life alone.

Dammit! This was nuts. Why should he feel guilty?

Sunny was saying something, and Adam held up a hand. "Hold it," he said. "I'm sorry, but I missed what you were saying. Will you begin again?"

She gave him a strange look, but went on. "I simply said that life was similar to the present, in so far as I've lived alone, longing for you."

"But you were not a virgin," he protested. "You've known a lover's possession."

"One." Sunny raised her index finger. "I indulged in a brief affair while I was in college." A faint smile touched her lips. "He reminded me of you."

Adam scowled. "You knew a man in college who looked like me?"

"No." Her denial was emphatic. "I knew a

man in college who reminded me of you...in a way.''

He pierced her with a narrow-eyed stare. ''In exactly what way, then?''

Her green eyes sparkled with a teasing light. ''Well, he wasn't nearly as handsome as you are.'' She paused.

Certain it was for effect, he didn't rise to her bait, only maintained his drilling stare.

''Nor as tall.'' She paused once more, the devilish glow brighter in her eyes.

He arched one eyebrow.

''Nor as fierce when upset or angry.''

''Nor as passionate?'' he prompted.

She laughed. ''That, either.''

''And you love it,'' he suggested.

''Yes,'' she readily admitted.

''Would do anything for it?''

''Probably,'' she confessed, sighing.

''Peel me a grape.''

Sunny's laughter filled the room—and Adam's heart.

Thirteen

She was actually going to do it.

Adam stared in astonished amusement as, still laughing, Sunny got up and walked to the small table. She slanted a look at him over her shoulder.

"Do you want a refill of coffee, most fearsome and mighty lord of all you survey?" Her tone was one of awed respect, her attitude servile.

Adam lost it; laughter roared from his throat. God, he loved this woman, her sense of humor, her passion, her joy of life…even her unwavering beliefs.

"Ah…no, thank you," he finally managed to choke out past his laughter. "I'd probably strangle on it."

"As you wish, my liege," she said demurely, lifting the tray and turning to come back to him.

Studying her, her gleaming eyes shielded by her partially lowered lids, her serenely composed features, the fluid suppleness of her movements, Adam felt the most incredible sensation of contentment filling all the nooks and crannies of his being.

It didn't matter, the conflict of beliefs between them—mostly inside him—the short amount of time they had known each other. What was time, anyway? None of it mattered, he realized with an illuminating burst of insight.

Within two days that felt like a lifetime, Adam knew he had fallen irrevocably in love with this woman who claimed she had loved him forever.

Adam blinked out of his reverie when he felt her set the fruit tray on his lap. Bemused, he didn't notice the small grape she held in her fingers. He opened his mouth to reveal his thoughts to her, confess his love for her.

Sunny struck with the speed of lightning. Her hand shot out, popping the grape into his mouth.

"Close your eyes and pretend it's peeled," she drawled, causing the tray to tilt precariously as she plopped down next to him "If you want one peeled, I suggest you peel it yourself...my lord."

Controlling an urge to laugh and dump the tray by pouncing on her delectable body, Adam raised one eyebrow into an arch of arrogant annoyance.

"Are you trying to resurrect Magnus the Head Hunter?"

"Ahh...Magnus..." Sunny gave him an enthralled look and a heavy sigh. "Such a fierce, passionate, magnificent lover," she said in simpering tones.

"You want fierce?" he growled.

"Actually, I want a piece of cheese," she retorted, spearing a chunk of the Swiss.

Laughing, bantering, they devoured every morsel on the tray and every last drop of the coffee.

Replete, they set the tray aside, then sat close together, heads resting on the back of the settee.

"I'm stuffed," Sunny said, groaning with satisfaction.

"Not completely...yet," Adam murmured, turning his head to smile at her with leering, lecherous intent.

"Behave yourself, Mr. Grainger," Sunny scolded, her lips quivering with amusement. "It's unseemly of you to make lewd suggestions to me at this advanced stage of our on-going, never-ending relationship."

"No kidding?" Adam pulled a wry expression, but inside his mind was working on the content of her jibe.

Their ongoing, never-ending relationship. In retrospect, he asked himself if there could by any stretch of credulity be some substance to the strange and unsettling visions or memory flashes or whatever he had experienced earlier while on the college campus.

Sunny believed without question or doubt.

So, also, did Charles Lawrence.

The thought of whom activated another question.

"The man who spoke to you the day we met," he said abruptly, noting the sudden surprise in her eyes. "The man you said was called Mr. White... this time."

Sunny frowned. "Yes. What about him?"

"His name is Charles Lawrence."

"I know." Her frown gave way to puzzlement. "But how did you learn his name?"

"I met him here in the lobby," he answered, amazed at the realization that it had been only the day before. Could it really have been just yesterday? he mused.

"And?" Sunny gave him a verbal nudge.

"What?" he asked, still pondering the seeming interactions of contracting and expanding time, his time, since he had first sighted Sunny strolling down the Palace Green.

"You said you met Mr. Lawrence," she reminded him, her voice shaded by the colors of hope and expectation.

"Oh...yeah." He shrugged. "He introduced himself and we had breakfast together."

Odd, that meeting. Had it been mere happenstance or could fate have had a hand in it? Adam reflected. Now, less than two days later, he couldn't recall tasting the food—or even ordering it, for that matter; he had been so startled by the man's story. And he recalled that with perfect clarity.

Stories. Both Sunny and Charles Lawrence had stories to tell, stories of past lives, past loves.

"Adam?"

He started, blinked, gave her a self deprecating smile. "Er...I was thinking."

"About what?" she probed, very gently.

"When you told me he had been here before, I had presumed you were referring to the present, current time." His eyes delved into the open green depths of hers. "But you weren't, were you?"

"No." She gave a quick shake of her head. "He told you, didn't he...about us, he and I, I mean?"

Alarm flared to vibrant life inside Adam. Sunny and Charles Lawrence? A sour, sick feeling invaded his stomach. His imagination went into overdrive. Had they been lovers at some distant period of time? Lawrence and...*his* Sunny?

"What about you and Lawrence," he demanded in a gritty teeth-bared snarl.

"Adam!" She laughed and her eyes took on a brilliance, as though a powerful light had been switched on inside them. "I do believe you're jealous," she crowed.

Adam grunted.

She relented. "He was my tutor," she explained, her glittering eyes revealing her delight. "During that oh-so-pampered-and-empty lifetime I told you about... The Charles Lawrence of today was Mr. James Carleton then, my very respectful and proper teacher."

"Oh." The sense of relief Adam felt was nearly unbearable, in light of his having endured a moment of almost insane jealousy over the mere possibility of Sunny being intimate with another man in a previous existence.

It *was* insane. Adam told himself. Unless... His thinking process came to a screeching halt on a preposterous idea. Unless he was on the verge of accepting...

Adam shook his head, but the thought refused to be banished. What if? What if... He was almost afraid to ask, and yet he had to know.

"Do you have any more stories to tell me?"

"Yes, many," she said, her voice softened with patience and compassion. "But for the present, I'll relate just one more, the most recent of my memory flashes."

Adam didn't wince at the term "flashes." How could he, having experienced them himself.

"When and where did this...lifetime take place?"

"Right here. Oh, not right here, in this motel, but here in Williamsburg, the original Williamsburg."

Naturally, Adam immediately thought of the

flashes he had had, but they had not been together then. With another sudden burst of insight, he knew that it had been Sunny he had been searching for at the time.

Logic followed that she had to be referring to yet another time in Virginia.

"And when did this take place?" he repeated.

"Before the revolution," she said. "During the time Patrick Henry was making himself heard."

No wonder she had remarked on the bust of the patriot in the lobby that first evening. She had known it was a good likeness of Patrick Henry.

Had that also been the reason he had felt drawn, been so riveted by the portrait of the man in the capitol building the other day?

Had he, perhaps, actually known the man, too?

The thought inspired a compelling sense of recognition in Adam…recognition and sheer awe.

"We were happy, then, but also disappointed."

"What?" With some difficulty, Adam refocused his sight and attention on Sunny. "I'm sorry, but I missed all of what you said. Did you say we were disappointed?"

"Yes." Sunny nodded. "Happy together, but disappointed by our failure to procreate."

"We couldn't have children?" While he posed it as a question, some inner knowledge knew he had no need to ask; he already knew the answer.

"No." Sunny's eyes, those incredible windows

into her thoughts and emotions, were sad. "It was my fault. I was barren."

"Because you were frightened." Again not a question, but absolute certainty.

Surprise flared to life in her eyes, surprise and shining hope. "How do you know that?"

How often had he asked himself that same question recently? Adam mused. How often had he avoided facing the answer? he chided himself. Had he deliberately closed himself off in his determination to remain logical, rational?

What would happen if he let himself go, opened up, accepted the possibility?

It happened swiftly.

It all came together, the memory flashes zipping through his mind, then pouring from his lips.

"There was an energy moving through the colonies. Many appeared infected by a spirit of revolt." Adam could no longer see Sunny as she was today. With his memory's eye, he saw her as she had been, every inch as beautiful, but not as bold and intrepid. Shy and uncertain, afraid of the future, that other Sunny had been terrified by the heady sense of independence permeating the land.

"Though I found that energy exciting, challenging, much as my former selves, the fierce Celt and Magnus, would have, the energy, the talk frightened you, frightened you so badly, you were terrified—at a deep, unconscious level—of bringing a child into the world. Unknowingly, you rendered yourself barren and unable to conceive.''

"Andrew." Barely a whisper.

He heard, and automatically responded. "Yes?"

A soft sigh. "You know."

"Yes, now I know." He had been Andrew, and the young student of over a hundred years before Andrew, and Magnus the Head Hunter, and the fierce Celt, and who knew how many others in between.

"And now that you know," she hesitated, moistened her lips, looked anxious. "Do you still resent me?"

That jolted Adam. "Resent you? I never did," he denied with soft vehemence.

"Yes, love, you did."

Yes, he had. Adam could feel the old emotion stirring, rising to the surface. It no longer had the power to effect his judgment. Well, how about that, he reflected with wry understanding. Living almost half of this lifetime in the pursuit of reasoned thinking and logic had been beneficial in more than the ways of commerce.

"Adam?" The tremor in Sunny's voice alerted him to the agony of uncertainty she was suffering.

"Do I still resent you?" he asked. "A secret resentment I had tried to hide from you, because you were so delicate, so fearful, so unsure?"

As if afraid to speak, she gave a quick, jerky nod.

"Have I been acting like a man who resents you?" He arched his brow. "A man harboring a secret?"

"No." She swallowed—it looked painful and tore at his heart. "But...but that was before you knew, before you remembered our time together."

"That's true." Adam nodded, then went on, "But it was also before I remembered our other times together. How I screamed with the pain and grief, when rather than live without me, you died with our child already dead within you. How you labored to present a son to please Magnus, after having labored to produce four daughters for him."

"You remember that, too?" she whispered.

"Yes, just now," he admitted, "It came to me in a flash." Smiling into her fabulous eyes, Adam reached for her, drawing her into the gentle protection of his embrace. "I remember something else, as well."

Sunny raised her tear-drenched eyes to his. "What do you remember, love?"

"I remember how you always called me love. And how much I have always loved you." Lowering his head, Adam kissed the tears from her cheeks. "How much I love you now." He brushed his lips over hers. "How I will continue throughout eternity to love you."

"Promise?" Sunny sniffed, and smiled.

"Do you continue to love me?" he countered, only half teasing, half terrified.

"With every fiber of every being," she vowed.

"As God is my witness, I promise to love you, only you," he renewed his ancient vow. "Throughout eternity."

Epilogue

It was the July Fourth weekend, and it was blazing hot in Virginia.

Sunny stood quiet and pensive in the Bruton Parish churchyard, in the pool of deep shade cast by a large, old magnolia tree.

Colonial Williamsburg was overflowing with a flood of tourists of all ages, all of whom had gathered in the restored area to celebrate the official anniversary of the country the founding fathers had named the United States of America.

Yet, while the surrounding area buzzed with the excited hum of humanity, calm serenity prevailed within the walled cemetery yard of the old church.

A few of the tourists ambled along the paths,

their voices hushed in deference to the past residents buried in the shaded cemetery.

While fully aware of the others, Sunny only had eyes for the tall man strolling the grounds, pausing here, then there to examine a headstone or marker, and where legible, read the inscriptions chiseled upon them.

Adam.

A tender smile curved Sunny's lips and she slid her palm over her extended belly, as if in tactile communication with the child growing inside her womb.

Adam, her child's father. How she loved him, had always loved him, would always love him, be he known as Adam or Andrew or Magnus or her fierce Celt or any other name—pronounceable or not.

Every so often in his wanderings, Adam's body would give a slight jolt and he would stretch out his hand to trace his fingers over an inscription.

At those times, Sunny's lips were tugged into a faint, sad smile, knowing he had read, recognized the scripted name of a former friend or acquaintance.

A pang of compassionate understanding pierced her each and every time, for he would turn to look at her, his expression one of pain and sorrow.

Sunny knew that expression, had felt the pain and sorrow during her own first examination of the inscriptions. But she knew, as well, that the pain and sorrow would pass. She knew the truth of the adage about time healing all wounds.

In the background, Sunny noted the crackling noise of exploding small fireworks, probably set off on the Palace Green by enthusiastic youngsters. She smiled in anticipation of the day her own child might be celebrating in the same way.

The crackling noise must have reached Adam, too. Returning her smile in near perfect communion, he turned to resume his stroll through the grounds.

Her gaze fastened on him, Sunny kept watch, her pulse rate increasing as Adam, almost as if guided, headed deeper into the cemetery yard.

Her breath caught in her throat when he came to halt along the outer side of the yard, near the farthest corner of the cemetery.

He went steel rigid, as if turned to stone.

Sunny knew why he stood transfixed.

She drew a quick, shallow breath when Adam bent forward, then crouched to peer intently at a long, flat, rectangular stone marker, raised but a few inches above the ground.

He crouched there, still and silent, for some minutes. Then, his broad shoulders heaving with a deeply indrawn breath, he rose, made a half turn toward her and held out a hand, mutely imploring her to come to him.

Leaving the relative coolness of the pool of shade, Sunny stepped into the searing July sunshine. Her bright smile rivaling the sparkling sun rays, she went to him, her own hand outstretched. She slid her palm into his, shivering from a thrill of delight when his hand curled around hers, warm, secure, protective.

Adam canted his head, directing her gaze to the old, barely legible inscriptions.

"Us," he murmured in an emotion-roughened voice.

"Yes," she whispered, matching his tone.

"Andrew Morgan," he read the script aloud in a hushed tone. "Beloved husband of Katherine." His eyes sought hers. "It's a pretty name."

"Yes." She nodded.

Shifting his gaze back to the stone, he continued to read aloud. "Katherine Morgan. Beloved wife of Andrew." He was quiet a moment, then he murmured, "You were, you know. Beloved, I mean. Even while I was resenting you, I loved you more than my own life."

"I know." Sunny could barely speak through the tears clogging her throat. "And even while I was living in fear of the future, I loved you more than my own life."

"I know." Smiling, he returned his attention to the stone, to read aloud the dates noted beneath the side-by-side names. His voice fading on the sultry air, he tilted his head to smile once again at her.

"We enjoyed a long life together."

"We'd have enjoyed it more if I had had the courage to trust you, your faith in the future, and given you the child I knew you so desperately longed for."

"No, love," he said, squeezing her hand in reassurance. "I wanted a child, yes, but my deepest desire then, as now, was for your well-being and happiness."

"Oh, Adam," Sunny cried on a pending sob. "I am happy, happy I found you again, happy to be carrying your child, so happy and so wildly in love with you."

With utter disregard for the curious eyes that might observe them, Adam drew her into his arms, tenderly careful of the precious burden she carried.

And there, in full view of God and man, Adam gave her the gift of his total acceptance.

"I love you, whoever you are, whoever you may be," he whispered. "Through all our seasons past, and all our seasons yet to come, I will love you."

* * * * *

MILLION DOLLAR SWEEPSTAKES
OFFICIAL RULES
NO PURCHASE NECESSARY TO ENTER

1. To enter, follow the directions published. Method of entry may vary. For eligibility, entries must be received no later than March 31, 1998. No liability is assumed for printing errors, lost, late, non-delivered or misdirected entries.

   To determine winners, the sweepstakes numbers assigned to submitted entries will be compared against a list of randomly, preselected prize winning numbers. In the event all prizes are not claimed via the return of prize winning numbers, random drawings will be held from among all other entries received to award unclaimed prizes.

2. Prize winners will be determined no later than June 30, 1998. Selection of winning numbers and random drawings are under the supervision of D. L. Blair, Inc., an independent judging organization whose decisions are final. Limit: one prize to a family or organization. No substitution will be made for any prize, except as offered. Taxes and duties on all prizes are the sole responsibility of winners. Winners will be notified by mail. Odds of winning are determined by the number of eligible entries distributed and received.

3. Sweepstakes open to residents of the U.S. (except Puerto Rico), Canada and Europe who are 18 years of age or older, except employees and immediate family members of Torstar Corp., D. L. Blair, Inc., their affiliates, subsidiaries, and all other agencies, entities, and persons connected with the use, marketing or conduct of this sweepstakes. All applicable laws and regulations apply. Sweepstakes offer void wherever prohibited by law. Any litigation within the province of Quebec respecting the conduct and awarding of a prize in this sweepstakes must be submitted to the Régie des alcools, des courses et des jeux. In order to win a prize, residents of Canada will be required to correctly answer a time-limited arithmetical skill-testing question to be administered by mail.

4. Winners of major prizes (Grand through Fourth) will be obligated to sign and return an Affidavit of Eligibility and Release of Liability within 30 days of notification. In the event of non-compliance within this time period or if a prize is returned as undeliverable, D. L. Blair, Inc. may at its sole discretion, award that prize to an alternate winner. By acceptance of their prize, winners consent to use of their names, photographs or other likeness for purposes of advertising, trade and promotion on behalf of Torstar Corp., its affiliates and subsidiaries, without further compensation unless prohibited by law. Torstar Corp. and D. L. Blair, Inc., their affiliates and subsidiaries are not responsible for errors in printing of sweepstakes and prize winning numbers. In the event a duplication of a prize winning number occurs, a random drawing will be held from among all entries received with that prize winning number to award that prize.

5. This sweepstakes is presented by Torstar Corp., its subsidiaries and affiliates in conjunction with book, merchandise and/or product offerings. The number of prizes to be awarded and their value are as follows: Grand Prize — $1,000,000 (payable at $33,333.33 a year for 30 years); First Prize — $50,000; Second Prize — $10,000; Third Prize — $5,000; 3 Fourth Prizes — $1,000 each; 10 Fifth Prizes — $250 each; 1,000 Sixth Prizes — $10 each. Values of all prizes are in U.S. currency. Prizes in each level will be presented in different creative executions, including various currencies, vehicles, merchandise and travel. Any presentation of a prize level in a currency other than U.S. currency represents an approximate equivalent to the U.S. currency prize for that level, at that time. Prize winners will have the opportunity of selecting any prize offered for that level; however, the actual non U.S. currency equivalent prize if offered and selected, shall be awarded at the exchange rate existing at 3:00 P.M. New York time on March 31, 1998. A travel prize option, if offered and selected by winner, must be completed within 12 months of selection and is subject to: traveling companion(s) completing and returning of a Release of Liability prior to travel; and hotel and flight accommodations availability. For a current list of all prize options offered within prize levels, send a self-addressed, stamped envelope (WA residents need not affix postage) to: MILLION DOLLAR SWEEPSTAKES Prize Options, P.O. Box 4456, Blair, NE 68009-4456, USA.

6. For a list of prize winners (available after July 31, 1998) send a separate, stamped, self-addressed envelope to: MILLION DOLLAR SWEEPSTAKES Winners, P.O. Box 4459, Blair, NE 68009-4459, USA.

Coming this July...

36 HOURS

Fast paced, dramatic, compelling... and most of all, passionate!

For the residents of Grand Springs, Colorado, the storm-induced blackout was just the beginning. Suddenly the mayor was dead, a bride was missing, a baby needed a home and a handsome stranger needed his memory. And on top of everything, twelve couples were about to find each other and embark on a once-in-a-lifetime love. No wonder they said it was 36 Hours that changed *everything!*

Don't miss the launch of 36 Hours this July with *Lightning Strikes* by bestselling author Mary Lynn Baxter!

Win a framed print of the entire 36 Hours artwork! See details in book.

Available at your favorite retail outlet.

Silhouette ®

™

New York Times **Bestselling Author**

REBECCA BRANDEWYNE

FOR GOOD OR FOR EVIL—
THE INSIDE STORY...

The noble Hampton family, with its legacy of sin and scandal, suffers the ultimate tragedy: the ruthless murder of one of its own.

There are only two people who can unravel the case—

JAKE SERINGO is the cynical cop who grew up on the mean streets of life;

CLAIRE CONNELLY is the beautiful but aloof broadcast journalist.

They'd parted years ago on explosive terms—now they are on the trail of a bizarre and shocking family secret that could topple a dynasty.

GLORY SEEKERS

The search begins at your favorite
retail outlet in June 1997.

<u>MIRA</u> **The brightest star in women's fiction.**

MRBGS

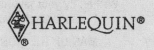